I0566347

Heather Higgins

tells True Love

to Kiss her Tatts

Bekki Diefendorf

Copyright © 2025 by Bekki Diefendorf

All rights reserved.

No portion of this book may be reproduced in any form without written permission from the publisher or author, except as permitted by U.S. copyright law. All characters and circumstances are fictional.

For my big sister

Contents

Tattoos are forever

My tatts are the first thing you'll notice.

You really can't help it. They aren't subtle.

Please, feel free to be distracted. Be intrigued. You can even be judgmental, if that's how you roll. I don't care. Just don't ask if you can touch them.

Spoiler alert: they feel like skin.

Moving on.

I don't have face tatts. My Mima made me promise, and a Mima promise is sacred.

Everywhere else though, yeah.

And every one tells a story.

Chapter 1

Poor Professor Higgins

"Professor Higgins! Wait!"

I keep walking. On the quad around me students take advantage of the gorgeous late summer day. The semester has just begun, and it's not yet time to worry about tests and essays. No, it's time to throw frisbees or sit in the shade with newly-made friends from the dorm. Not long ago that would have been me reclining on a blanket, earbuds playing, book in hand.

Now my only goal is to escape to my cave of an office in the basement of Caseman Hall.

"Professor Higgins!"

Crap. The voice is closer. I catch a pointed glance from a passing colleague and stop with a deep inhale. Ignoring students is frowned upon here at Springvale University.

Turning, I scan the quad for the person attached to the voice. About twenty feet away I spot a vaguely familiar, bright-cheeked coed waving her arm frantically. Has she been chasing me since I left *Intro to Linguistics*?

I scowl down at the mustard yellow heels that were so irresistible this morning. The heels that forced me to walk on the concrete pathways and slowed my progress enough that I've been caught by a student willing to sacrifice her personal dignity in a mad dash across the lawn. I'm sure there's a lesson in there about the price of vanity, but I still don't regret wearing them. We all prioritize.

"Judas," I mutter beneath my breath.

The shoes don't reply.

"What's that?" a voice asks.

I look up to find the young woman with the lack of dignity standing before me. Man, she's fast.

"What's what?" I ask.

"Did you say something?"

I stare at her blankly.

"Never mind," she says between raspy breaths. She's bent over, one hand in the air in a "just a second" gesture that I can't imagine ever giving a professor. "I'm so glad I caught you, Professor Higgins," the girl pants out. "I have a question."

I contain my sigh, allowing the beauty of the day to infuse me with peace. I will give this student my full attention, and then I will retreat to my office and lock out the world.

Unfortunately the young woman before me is taking forever to catch her breath. Not an athlete, this one. I force myself not to tap my lovely heels. When my raised eyebrow elicits no response, I resort to language.

"Are you ok?" I ask.

4

"Jaynie."

Jaynie? This student thinks I care what her name is? That's cute.

"Yes, Jaynie," I say. I force the corners of my mouth to flex upwards. "What's your question?"

"Well, Professor Higgins." She stops speaking abruptly, startled as a guy on a skateboard skirts past us a touch too close.

"Jaynie?" I regain her attention. She blinks at me.

"Oh, yeah," she says. "Should I call you Professor Higgins or Doctor Higgins?" Jaynie asks. "Because you have your PhD, right?"

"I do."

"So which should I call you?"

This is why I don't talk to students.

"Either will be fine." I do my best imitation of a teacher who cares, even going so far as to pause before nodding and continuing my walk towards my office. To my chagrin, Jaynie walks beside me. I stop again, unwilling to lead this young woman back to my sanctuary.

"Is there something else?" I ask.

"Yes. My question."

Apparently how to address me was not the answer she sought. I raise one eyebrow. After one more long indrawn breath, Jaynie lets out a rush of words.

"When you assigned us to watch *My Fair Lady*, did you do it to get the obvious 'Professor Higgins' references out of the way, or because you believe that movie's a great way to introduce us to the subtle societal interplay that comes from dialectical differences?"

Huh. I take a moment to re-access. This Jaynie, despite her willingness to chase me across the quad and rambling vocal style, may end up learning something in my class after all.

"Perhaps I did it for neither reason," I say.

I did it for both.

Young Jaynie is undeterred.

"Then why did you do it?" she asks.

I pause, considering the lawn around me filled with students like Jaynie. Young minds ready for molding.

"That, Jaynie," I say, granting her the dubious honor of remembering her name, "is a question I'm not going to answer." I force a smile and wish her a good afternoon.

Not looking back, I walk towards the sanctuary of Caseman Hall.

Tattoo 1: Elanor

I did not become a professor because of an altruistic desire to impact the mindsets of a generation. There was no noble goal before me.

No. I became a professor because after six years of post-secondary education my writing career consisted of three fantasy manuscripts and a stack of rejection notices nearly as deep as my student loans.

Why fantasy, you ask? Maybe because my father, my real father, left me a worn copy of *The Lord of the Rings* marked with notes and highlights throughout the way someone pious might annotate a Bible.

Maybe because entering another world has always been easier than living in this one.

Maybe I just think Fae guys are hot.

Or maybe it's D.) all of the above.

What I can tell you for sure is that from the time I was nine and first made it through that copy of *The Lord of the Rings*, I planned to be the next J.R.R. Tolkien. Middle Earth was so much a part of my being that I celebrated my eighteenth birthday with my first tattoo, an Elanor flower on my forearm.

Tiny, lovely and hidden away in an elven kingdom, the Elanor was my spirit flower. Gold and silver. Bright and shiny. An optimistic blossom, like I was at the time. I designed the tattoo myself, and never regretted it.

Unlike those aforementioned student loans.

Chapter 2

Nemesis

I step out of the elevator onto the cold, speckled tile of the basement corridor. My glorious, traitorous heels dangle from one hand.

(Pause for a second. I hear you. I'm aware that it's gross to walk in a public hallway barefoot. And I promise, this isn't normal for me. But from the time Jaynie accosted me on the lawn, my shoe straps have been slicing the backs of my ankles to the point that not even the threat of foot fungus is an adequate deterrent.)

Above me a fluorescent light flickers. This forgotten section of Caseman Hall has yet to be retrofitted with LED's, and the ceiling is lined with murder rectangles of the type normally found in dentist offices and 1980's horror films. We won't even discuss the confidence hit I take every time I see myself in the reflective surface of the elevator doors.

I'm halfway down the beige on beige hallway when I hear a sound that chills my blood.

Angry voices . . . A gunshot . . . An ominous thud . . . ?

Nope. Not that kind of book.

Besides this is worse.

Tinkling laughter ricochets down the corridor.

That's right. It's the first week of school and Darcy's groupies have found us already.

I say "us" in the loosest sense. They've found him. Unfortunately Professor Darcy Delancey's office is directly across the hall from mine. Which means that my refuge, the tiny basement cell I employ for power naps and avoidance, has been breached in record time.

"I still don't understand why he was so hard on Emma," says the young female voice spilling from Professor Delancey's open doorway. "She was just being honest."

My office is right there. Just a few more steps . . .

"Well, Megan, in order to truly understand the depth of Emma's error, you need to understand the class system of the day and the unwritten rules of etiquette that governed it."

Nope. I can't let it go, even if Delancey doesn't deserve the intervention. I poke my head into his pristine office.

"I couldn't help overhearing," I say. "Might I add something?"

I love watching the annoyance lines form around Darcy's crystal blue eyes. His pleasant expression looks genuine, if you don't know better. He'd never be unprofessional around a student. His eyes dart from the heels in my hands to my bare feet and his mouth twitches downwards for the briefest of moments.

"Professor Higgins, always a delight," Delancey says, leaning forward to rest his elbows on his desk. "I appreciate your insight, although this isn't exactly your area of expertise."

"Actually, I think it is," I say with a smile. I'm going for enigmatic, but it borders on fierce. My smiles tend that way around him.

"Megan?" I say, turning to the young woman who's been trying, unsuccessfully, to make her tiny skirt cover a bit more of her thighs. "Did you watch the Gwyneth Paltrow version or *Clueless*?"

Megan's eyes go wide. "I'm not sure what you mean," she stammers. Her gaze darts to Darcy. To his credit, he doesn't intervene.

"Which did you watch?" I ask, adding steel to my voice. "It's early in the semester, and you have time to read the book before you're tested on it. You might as well fess up now."

She holds my gaze for a moment, then her shoulders slump.

"*Clueless*," she says.

"Indeed," I answer. "How about you not waste Professor Delancey's time if you haven't read the book, yeah?"

"Yeah, ok," she says, picking up her backpack as she stands. With one last glance Darcy's direction, she mumbles a goodbye and scurries past me into the hallway.

I wait until she's nearly at the elevator, then I turn towards my own office.

"You're welcome," I tell Darcy over my shoulder.

"For what?"

I pause, looking back. The man seems genuinely puzzled.

"I just saved you from wasting your breath and your precious time on a student who couldn't even be bothered to complete the assignment," I say.

"Hmmmm," he says. So annoying.

"What does that mean?"

"Nothing. Only that, as a professor, I wouldn't think you'd see interacting with students as a waste of time."

I scoff.

11

"Oh, Fitzwilliam, it's like you don't know me at all."

I'm turning the key in my office door when Delancey calls my name.

"Professor Higgins."

He times this for maximum inconvenience. I know he does. Pasting a smile on my face, I backtrack the few steps to his doorway.

"Yes, Professor Delancey?" My voice is as sweet as cotton candy at the county fair.

"How did you know Megan hadn't read the book?" he asks.

"How did you not know?" I ask back.

"Please," he says, "explain."

"Fine," I say on a huff. "It was clear *Megan* hadn't read the book because pretty people are always given a pass, even when they act like mountain trolls. She'd obviously seen a pretty version of Emma."

"Huh," he says. Nothing else as this new concept sinks into his pretty head. Hopefully he's re-evaluating his whole existence through this lens.

Whatever.

I cross the hall to the safety of my little box, let myself in, and settle down for a nap.

Tattoo 9: Larkspur

Professor Darcy Delancey is the only straight, American male I know to focus his career around the writings of Jane Austen.

I'm sure he would have preferred to be named Fitzwilliam, for authenticity's sake, but in an ironic twist of fate, his mother never read Pride and Prejudice. She really should have named him "Collin."

How do I know this? Because Darcy's mother and mine were sorority sisters. Both were old money, attending the college their forebears had patronized for generations. It only made sense that they hit it off.

Both women married right out of college, were the bests at each other's weddings, and got pregnant within the year.

In another universe, Darcy and I would have grown up together.

In this universe, my father died of a rare form of cancer when I was nine months old.

There's a video of Darcy and me, age two and a half. I'm wearing a lacy white dress and scattering rose petals down the aisle at my mom and step-dad's wedding. Darcy walks beside me in a suit, a tiny pillow with plastic rings strapped to his wrist. In the video you can watch his expression progress from surprised to annoyed to downright fed up as he looks from my basket to the pink trail on the floor behind us and back again.

Finally it's more than tiny Darcy can take. He grabs the basket, wrenching it from my unsuspecting fists, and tears up the aisle to where his mother waits in her matron of honor gown.

Did I chase him? You bet I did. Did I tear my basket from his hands and then rip the pillow off his wrist and throw it as hard as I could? Oh yeah.

Because two and a half year old me was a badass, and you didn't mess with her flower basket. Fist bump, past self. I honor you.

The thing, though, that's most important about this story, is that Darcy has no idea that girl was me.

Crazy, right?

We moved after the wedding, following my new step-dad's job across the country. Our moms got together for girl trips, sans children, and I didn't see Darcy Delancey again until the first day of new staff orientation at Springvale University.

I knew he'd be there. My mother told me in the midst of dress fittings and cake tastings for my brother's upcoming Big Day. Apparently Darcy's mother didn't think to mention me.

To be fair, I don't share my mother's last name. "Higgins" is from my dad. But you'd think in the five years since we've worked together it might have come up.

But no. Darcy Delancey only sees what's on the surface. And my surface is beautiful. But not in the way he acknowledges beauty.

I wasn't hoping we could be friends, or that I would know someone, anyone, on my first day in a brand-new place with a brand new job.

14

That there would be some sort of comfort or protection in not being alone.

Of course I wasn't.

But I also wasn't expecting Assistant Professor Darcy Delancey, the son of my mother's life-long best friend, to look at me blankly, force a smile, and continue to box me out of the conversation he was having with the faculty dean.

That weekend, after drinks with a new friend from the physics department, I got a tattoo to commemorate Darcy's loss of favor forever.

Sure, it wasn't the most mature reason to ink myself, and it hurt like hell. But the lovely, and highly toxic, larkspur flower dripping it's poison petals along the inside of my middle finger always makes me smile.

Chapter 3

Ride or Die

"Honey, I'm home," I holler as I step into to the two-bedroom bungalow I share with my ride or die, partner in crime, non-sexual soulmate.

Olivia and I met at new staff orientation. After my failed attempt at conversation with Darcy, I found a seat near a hoodie-clad figure in the back row. In a way, Darcy did me a favor.

Olivia became my default partner in ice breaker activities, and she and I have been inseparable ever since. We moved into an adorable bungalow purchased by her parents over our first winter break and then weathered Covid in our own little bubble, at first teaching lectures via Zoom and shortly after, due to our non-tenured newbie status, basking in furlough and unemployment.

Besides some surface changes, slightly more professor-ish clothing choices, a few more tattoos, we're basically the same as we were then.

Did I mention that we're both turning thirty this year, within two days of each other? Yep.

Will we party hard to celebrate the end of the twenties? Yes, we will. If you consider pairing red wine with Mexican takeout and fig newtons while watching every episode of *Community* a party. Which I do.

I know I've mentioned my tatts, but hopefully the ink on my skin didn't make you cram me into a "wild child" stereotype, because if you did you'd be dealing with a lot of unfulfilled assumptions right about now. I want you to do this.

First: pretend I'm not covered in tattoos.

Second: take into account the following facts:

1- I am a linguistics professor.

2- My best friend is a physics professor.

3- I write non-successful fantasy novels in my spare time.

4- When not writing non-successful fantasy novels, I'm trading critiques with my online non-successful fantasy novel writing friends.

5- My nemesis is a man who's obsessed with Jane Austen.

Got it? So that picture of me that's in your head right now? That's me on the inside. Assume those things. Then add the tatts. Because I am badass, at least on the surface.

Olivia doesn't answer my shout, which means she isn't home (unlikely on a Friday night), she's showering, or she's asleep. I put my bag down on the kitchen table and walk the short hall to our rooms. I poke my head into Olivia's bedroom, but she isn't there. The bathroom door beside me is open.

No Olivia. Huh.

Feeling a bit lost, I wander into my own room and pull my phone from my pocket to text her.

Where u b?

Intriguing.

I tag Olivia's text with a thumbs up. This is the perfect window to work on the fourth final draft of my latest novel, [Insert Fascinating Title Here}. (I'm lousy at titles. You come up with something you think is cool and pretend I said it, ok?)

Wandering to the kitchen, I retrieve my laptop. I resist the pull of the fridge, mainly because I know there's nothing compelling in it. The sofa calls to me like old man willow luring the hobbits into its clutches, but I stay strong. If I really want to write, my best chance is the uncomfortable desk chair in my bedroom.

I make it to said desk chair and I'm feeling good. Professional authorship, here I come.

But before I start editing, I'm going to check in, really quick, to see if anyone I know is online tonight.

Which is how I end up debating the merits of creating your own language for a novel vs borrowing from an already established linguistic system. I don't know why Keto95 hasn't just bowed to my obviously superior knowledge in this area. Hello, I have a PhD.

Apparently arguing online has the same affect on time as having fun, because after what seems like moments I hear the front door open and close.

"Olivia?" I call.

The sound she makes defies my powers of phonetic transcription. I look up from the laptop screen to find my best friend standing in the doorway.

"What happened?"

18

It's all I can get out before I start laughing.

Olivia scowls, purses her lips, and stomps into the bathroom.

I hop out of my chair and follow close behind her.

"I'm sorry," I say to the closed bathroom door. "Really, I am."

I'm sure Olivia can hear the grin I'm trying to suppress. She flings the door open.

"If I have to spend one more hour with Andrew Chu," she says, "someone is going to die."

I reach out slowly and pull forward a piece of hair that's escaped her long ponytail.

"Is this burnt?" I ask.

"Yes," she says. "Yes it is. And you should probably wash your hand. I'm not sure I got all of the acid off."

I look down at my fingertips. Are they tingling?

My eyes dart back to Olivia's face. She's smirking and shaking her head.

"You make it so easy," she says.

"Not funny," I say as she closes to bathroom door behind her. "I'm going to order Chinese in honor of Andrew."

"Please, no." Her voice is muffled. "Greek? Mexican? Thai?"

I think of ordering something bland and aristocratic in honor of Darcy.

"Thai's good," I say instead.

Tattoo 8: Mima's Butterfly

My Mima has always been the angel on my shoulder.

When I wanted to say "screw it all," she'd say, "Not all, darling."

The last year of my MBA was spent writing in her room at the Sunny Days Facility for Elder Care. She'd sleep. She'd wake up and ask me who I was. Sometimes she'd ask me who she was. But every once in a while, she'd know. And she'd smile and call me to her side and look me in the eye and say "Heather, you're a good girl. It's all going to be just fine."

And I'd believe her.

Mima died two weeks before I finished my MBA. It started a downhill slide for me that culminated in "the incident" at my brother's rehearsal dinner and nearly total estrangement from my family.

Mima never would have let that happen.

I wear a butterfly tattoo in her honor, the only good thing to come out of that season of my life. Blue, white, and black, it flutters on my right shoulder blade amidst a smattering of flowers. Mima believed in rebirth after death, and in my best moments I believe with her.

Chapter 4

The pop-up that changed my life

My professor life doesn't touch Saturday. Saturday is for me.

I don't sleep in. I think I mentioned being a napper, yeah? It's so much better that way.

That's why, on Saturday at 4:43 am, I saw it. The pop-up that would change my life.

Jane, Reimagined- **Short Story Contest**
10 finalists will be included in our annual publication.
Grand prize: $500 and an agent 1 on 1 with Carmen Alexander.

Carmen Alexander . . . Only the agent who represents three of my four favorite authors of all time. (OK, not of all time. Of now. She doesn't represent the dead.)

Carmen Alexander, also known as "the Queen-maker." She finds new authors and turns them into genre goddesses.

Oh, Carmen . . . This is destiny.

But, wait . . .

I've clicked on the pop-up and what do I see staring back at me? The crystal blue eyes of Darcy Delancey.

Fignuts.

Beside his picture is a quote. "Jane Austen will always be an integral part of our literary consciousness."

I can't help rolling my eyes at screen Darcy. The pretention runs thick in this one.

As I take in the rest of the site, it becomes clear that *Jane, Reimagined* is a fan-girl site for Jane Austen lovers. I suppose that answers why Delancey's photo is on it. The boy is pretty if you don't know him.

Whatever.

I lean forward on my elbows, the bottoms of my palms holding me up by the cheekbones as I stare at the webpage.

I love Jane Austen. I mean, who doesn't. Such wit. Heroines that are just as relatable today as they were two hundred plus years ago. True love winning in the end.

But it's not my genre, you know? It's not WHAT I WRITE.

Oh, but Carmen Alexander . . .

I scour the rest of the website. There are no more references to Delancey. Nothing to suggest he has any connection with this organization beyond being decorative and quotable.

I sigh.

5,000 words isn't that many, really . . .

And no one will ever have to know.

Tattoo 3: Bandit

When I was little, I had an imaginary pet named "Bandit." He was a racoon who would sneak into the treats after mom said I couldn't have any, or leave the craft supplies a mess instead of cleaning up. He really was a very cheeky little rascal.

I bet you can guess where nineteen year old me put his tatt.

Chapter 5

The Cranky Bean

"Good afternoon, Professor Higgins."

I'm nearly to the front of an exceptionally long line at The Cranky Bean, our university's on-campus purveyor of caffeinated beverages and over-priced baked goods.

Professor Darcy Delancey has just announced his presence in that formal way of his that reminds me we are colleagues, not friends.

"Can I buy your coffee today?" he asks.

And this is when I really wish I hadn't been so wrapped up in my own thoughts about that stupid Jane Austen writing contest. Because I have no idea if Darcy has been behind me this entire time and I've been unintentionally ignoring him, or if he just cut the line and he's offering to buy me coffee for not calling him out on it.

I'm going to have to go with my gut on this one and say that, despite all of his entitlement and condescension, Darcy's professionalism wouldn't allow him to cut in line, particularly where students might see.

"Professor Delancey," I finally say. "I didn't even see you there. What a kind offer, but it's not needed."

"I insist," he says. We've reached the counter and before I can stop him, he's ordering for both of us.

"I'll have Moroccan Mint tea, extra hot," he says, "and my colleague here will have an almond-milk pistachio latte with light whipped cream."

I'm not sure whether to be annoyed that he ordered for me or flattered that he got it right. I could probably be annoyed by both if I tried.

"Is that all?" asks the cashier. He has an eyebrow piercing and almost as many tattoos as I do. He gives me a look that says "you're seriously with this guy?" I roll my eyes and he smirks.

"I'll take a cookie, too," I say, smiling sweetly at Darcy, "since you're buying."

"But of course," he says. "Whatever you'd like."

"Which do you recommend?" I ask the cashier.

"I don't eat sugar," he says.

Just when I thought there was potential.

"I'll take the Mexican Hot Cocoa cookie," I say.

"You got it."

Darcy pays and we join the crowd gathered near the pick-up counter.

"Are you heading back to the offices after this?" Darcy asks.

I had been, but I'm guessing that's his destination, and I don't want to encourage him to walk with me.

"Just came from there," I say. "It was putting me to sleep, so I thought I'd caffeinate and then work outside the rest of the afternoon."

"That's a marvelous idea," Darcy says. "I don't know how they expect us to do anything productive in that basement." His shudder is comically exaggerated, and my mouth is smiling without my consent before his next words freeze it in place.

"Mind if I join you?"

The barista calls Darcy's name, and he retrieves our drinks while I frantically attempt to process what just happened.

Did Darcy just suggest we hang out? Technically, it would still be two colleagues working, but I'm much more comfortable in my own little lair with a murder hallway between us.

Besides, I'm supposed to be writing a modern romance about a Jane Austen heroine. There's no way I'm letting Darcy into my subconscious on this one, regardless of how hot Hugh Grant was as Edward Ferrars. (Yes. I've taken the time to decide which Jane Austen character Darcy would have been, and while I wish he were a Willoughby, or even a Fitzwilliam, the resemblance to both Edward and young Hugh is too striking to ignore.)

Darcy walks back, smirking as he hands me the cup. Looking down, I see the name "Benji" and a phone number on the side in black sharpie.

"Not timid, I'll give him that," Darcy says.

I look towards the counter and Benji does that cool-guy chin lift that's been annoying me since junior high. I would laugh if Darcy wasn't beside me.

"Benjamin, right?" he asks. "Smart kid. Aced my 'Regency Janes' class last semester."

"Augh," I say. "I have never felt so old." Darcy laughs, and I join him. If I didn't know better, I'd think we could be friends. Then I glance at the larkspur on the finger of the hand holding my cup. See, that's what reminders are there for.

"I think I'm actually going to head home rather than work outside," I say. "There are too many distractions here, and I've got a deadline." He doesn't need to know the deadline is not at all work-related.

Darcy nods. "Of course," he says. "Enjoy your weekend."

"You too. And thanks for the coffee."

"Anytime."

Chapter 6
The heroine

It's harder than you'd think to write a regency heroine into a modern context. My latte and cookie are long gone, and so is the feeling in my right foot as I adjust my position, stretch, and finally decide to take a break and make popcorn.

Of course my first thought was Elizabeth. Whose isn't? But it's repetitive. She was a modern heroine over two hundred years ago, and there isn't enough hubris in the world to convince me I could write her as well as Jane did.

Emma? I just can't. If I put her into a modern context, I might run her over with a bus, *Mean Girls* style.

Marianne? She might as well be one of the students in Darcy's office with their big eyes and big dreams about to be destroyed by the big bad real world. As much as they annoy me, I don't want to write that. It was bad enough to have to live it. And her sister, Elinor . . . oh man, I wish I could like her more, but if someone was about to screw over my little brother that way, I'd be stepping in. Then again, that didn't work out so well for me.

Lady Susan is more villain than heroine.

Fanny Price, with her timid nature, would get even less respect today than she did in Austen's time.

And then there's Anne.

Anne Elliot from *Persuasion*. Oh, we loves her. We loves her. Smart and kind and over-looked. Maybe modern Anne needs a tattoo or two. Or four.

Tattoo 10: The Lotus Flower

The lotus flower is a universal symbol of strength, resilience and new beginnings.

It was also one final f-you to a society that would never accept me before I moved on forever.

It's not my least conventional tattoo, but it was the first that couldn't be ignored or covered up. Not when it was so prominently displayed on my neck in all its pink and black glory.

I woke up with it the morning after my brother's rehearsal dinner.

The woman my brother was marrying, Kitty, was a Southern bell who'd graduated just in time to supplement her B.A. in marketing with an M.R.S. into our family. She was the daughter my mother always wanted. Her make-up was tasteful, her blonde highlights never showed roots, and her designer jeans fit just so. She always had the perfect words, and she used them to say the exact opposite of what she really meant.

"Heather, that butterfly is such a beautiful tribute to Mima. I'm so glad you got it before the wedding so it could show beneath the straps of your bridesmaid dress." Here she bares her straight, white teeth. "It's really too bad they don't do any pictures from the back."

She fit my brother's life perfectly, but he deserved better.

My baby brother, heir apparent to my step-father's disposable tableware empire, finished his Ivy league degree in three years with the help of advanced placement options. Now he would marry and step into the rest of his life as the prince of plasticware. He and his lovely bride would have equally lovely children who'd play cello in the youth symphony and excel at lacrosse. Their lives would be perfect until it came out that Kitty was banging her yoga instructor, just like she had the best man, and then they'd have to split the lawyer fees and the entire forking corporation.

This wasn't my speech at the rehearsal dinner verbatim, but you get the gist.

You don't mock a Mima tattoo then give me alcohol and a microphone unless you want to regret it. Especially not if you have secrets.

Chapter 7

Thank you for your submission

I received a form letter the day I submitted my story. Now, as I click on the email from CR4@janereimagined.com, I expect an update. A rejection, if my track record is an indicator. But that's not what this is. This is . . . personal.

From: CR4@janereimagined.com
To: AnneElliot2024@gmail.com
Dear Ms. E,

First, let me make it clear that I have no influence on the outcome of the Jane, Reimagined writing contest to which you submitted Persuaded. All decisions regarding both the short and long lists and the grand prize winner are made by the panel of judges whose credentials are listed on the website.

That said, as part of the initial screening process, I have read close to seventy entries, and my mind keeps returning to your story. I've always loved Anne Elliot, and in your words I found a kindred spirit. It is clear that you, also, understand what it means to be alone amongst those who should be closest to you. Your conclusion was heart-wrenching, insightful, and provocative.

I've crossed a line with "kindred spirit," but I can't seem to make myself delete it. So I won't send this. I don't think I ever really intended to. Ah, but hope springs forth undesired, does it not. That need to connect . . .

But not today.

Sincerely,

F.W.

I read it again. Then another time. It's clear F.W. never meant to send this. I should ignore it. Pretend I never received it.

But I understand that need to connect. I don't know what I would have done if Olivia hadn't entered my life when she did. This really is no different than chatting with my fantasy friends online. Just a different genre of lit nerd.

And really, none of them has ever called my writing heart-wrenching, insightful, and provocative. How can I resist?

I at least owe F.W. a reply.

To: AnneElliot2024@gmail.com

From: CR4@janereimagined.com

Dear F.W.

I believe you sent the email above in error, and the most polite thing to do would be to ignore it completely. However, my writer's vanity won't allow it.

Thank you so much for your kind words. Like you, Anne has always been my favorite. As undervalued as Fanny Price, without the annoying name and shyness. This was my first attempt to write in this genre (I usually write fantasy), but I believe Anne could inspire anyone.

Though I know you didn't intend to reach out, I'm glad you did. The connection we crave must be found where it can.

Ugh. That sounds so cryptic. Screw it. If they want connection, I'll give them connection. If they run scared, so be it.

I've never felt like I fit in. Maybe it's because my mother "married beneath her," according to the rules of her society. My dad was an athlete, good enough to get a scholarship, but not enough to go pro. He died before I was a year old, and my mom remarried when I was two. I don't blame her. Life isn't easy for single moms. At the risk of sounding entirely Austenian, though, I swear he married her because she was a societally appropriate choice and he needed an heir.

My step-father's not a bad person, but there's always been a difference for him between me and my brother. I assume it's because I'm not actually his, but it could be that I'm the girl. It also didn't help that I have zero interest in business or making the "right" friends. If you looked up "daddy issues" on Wikipedia you'd probably find my picture, but I haven't taken the time to pay a therapist to make it official.

Well, that's enough of me oversharing. To be fair, you started it.
Ms. E.

I hit send before I can have second thoughts.

Tattoo 4: Harold and the Purple Crayon

My brother is engaged again. I found out on Instagram, where I follow him under a fake account with Olivia's picture.

My brother was born Harold Ashford Randolf III. For a couple years we called him Baby Harry, but then came that magical day when I read him his new favorite book, *Harold and the Purple Crayon*. He was Harold after that. And he was my shadow. I was his person, and he was mine.

In fifth grade Harold met Anthony. Harold hadn't made many friends to that point, and when he wanted to go by "Ash" because it made their names match, we didn't think much of it. Ash and Ant. Mom called them "the battery boys" for their AA status and endless energy. By college their slogan had changed to "Alcohol Anywhere," and my shy, sweet brother had vanished, along with any remembrance that I was once his favorite.

I don't know if anyone without a younger sibling can understand the fiery possessiveness that comes when you hold a tiny baby in your own little arms and find out he's your family now and will be forever. Or how badly it burns when you realize that isn't true.

I know I should have handled it differently.

Mima's death and my wretched new job and the alcohol are just excuses.

Somehow I was the only one who noticed how Ant looked at Kitty when my brother wasn't watching.

"I saw her first, you know," Ant would say, with a laugh. But it always made me uncomfortable.

Ant would throw his arm over Kitty's shoulder and grin down at her. She'd shrug him off with a forced smile. I thought she was sensing what I was, the inherent jealousy underlying so many of Ant's comments over the years.

Maybe she was. I don't know the details of their story. The whys or how oftens. I don't even know if love was involved, or if it was just attraction.

What I do know is that they shared a room at the Grand hotel in Phoenix when Kitty was supposed to be home visiting her family in Atlanta.

I know this because I watched them from an alcove as they made out in the lobby before leaving through two separate exits.

After half an hour spent attempting to deny what I'd seen and mingle at the Fantasy Writers of America convention, I excused myself and went to the check-out desk. *My poor sister was at the airport without her driver's license, and she thought she might have left it in the room. Anthony Clark and Kitty Spencer. That's right, they checked out this morning. Oh no. Housekeeping's already been there and there was no license. Thank you so much for your time. I need to call her. I don't know what she's going to do . . .*

I did call her. She gushed over what a great time she was having with her nieces and nephews. I really would need to come to Atlanta with her one day.

I called Ash, but it went to voicemail, and I didn't leave a message. We'd both be home for Easter, where I could tell him in person. I wasn't sure he'd believe me, but I had to try.

Kitty came home with him, her diamond engagement ring sparkling from her finger. They were going to marry quickly, this coming fall, so Mima could be there.

Then Mima died.

I didn't attend my MBA commencement. It was a week after the funeral, and I just couldn't. Mom didn't press. She was already dealing with her mother's death, her son's graduation and the upcoming wedding. An MBA was just a stepping stone to a doctorate. It could be ignored.

My step-father got me the assistant professor job at Springvale University. I would have fought him about it, but I couldn't fight anyone just then. I barely remember the interviews, so it's a good thing they were a formality.

That summer was a blur of fittings and tastings and packing. My step-father's assistant found me an apartment near campus and signed my lease.

In the midst of it all, Ash was always in the back of my mind. Ant and Kitty and Ash. I needed to tell him. Surely I did. But I'd put it off. Cave. Rationalize. *He looks so happy. Maybe it was just the once. Maybe it's over.*

But that night, at the rehearsal dinner, as I saw Kitty skim the back of her hand along Ant's arm as she passed by, I knew. Even as drunk as I was, I knew it wasn't over.

Would Ash have believed me that night if I'd pulled him aside and told him what I saw? I'll never know. Because after my drunken toast, into the stunned silence of the crowd, Ant finally lost it.

"I saw her first, damn it," he shouted, jumping to his feet. "You knew I wanted her."

My brother pushed back from the table, face contorted and throat working overtime as he looked from his best friend to his fiancé. Then he stood, and threw the kind of punch I'd never imagined him capable of. Ant sprawled to the ground. Ash stood over him, panting hard, then fast-walked, ultimately ran, out a side exit.

Kitty looked from my brother's fleeing figure to Ant on the carpet at her feet, then knelt down to push the hair back from Ant's face. He said something low I couldn't hear, and she started crying and nodding.

It made my heart sick. I followed my brother's path to the exit, but by the time I made it through the door, he was gone.

So I slid down against the wall, put my head in my hands, and wept.

If I could go back, I'd do it differently. But I'd still do it. Because my little brother deserves a woman who will love him and build a life with him, even if I'm not part of it.

This new girl on Instagram looks kind. Something in her eyes, or in my wishful thinking. Even in the ring picture, her nails aren't perfect, and that makes me like her more. Maybe one day she and I can be friends.

What was it F.W. said about undesired hope?

My brother was my fourth tattoo, right after Bandit. Harold with his purple crayon draws a crescent moon on my calf. So I guess, in a way, my brother will always be with me.

Chapter 8

Mirror, mirror

You might think that declaring Darcy my nemesis after he chose to ignore me, a complete stranger, at a single social function, is a bit extreme. And sure, looking back I could agree with you.

But then there was the conversation I overheard between him and his mother the Monday following the wedding disaster. You know, the one that split my family and destroyed my relationship with one of the most important people in my life.

If I didn't already have a hate tattoo for Darcy, I'd have gotten one that Monday.

Let me paint the scene.

Imagine the light has changed to signal a flashback. The world looks hazy, tinged with sepia, despite September sunshine. The edges are fuzzy, the sound muted.

I'm younger. A gauzy teal scarf floats around my neck, protecting my newly-acquired lotus tattoo from damaging UV rays.

As a brand new professor, I don't yet have an auto-pilot to engage for seminars. Which means that all morning my mind was focused on the torment of teaching rather than the fact that Ash has blocked not just my phone number but all of my socials.

I'm in my head, so I've been taking the same route across the quad as Darcy for a while before it registers. To be clear, I'm not following him, despite being behind him. This is entirely on whoever scheduled our classes and office hours for the same general times and locations.

Darcy, on the phone, is oblivious to my presence.

"Mom, surely you're being dramatic," he says. "It couldn't have been that bad." He's quiet, looking down at his apple watch before replying. "Well, then, I'm glad I missed it . . . No, Mom. I couldn't have made it regardless. There was a faculty dinner Friday night and all new hires were required to attend."

That's what caught my attention. Did I miss a mandatory faculty dinner Friday night, or is Darcy the kind of man who lies to his mother?

Obviously I couldn't have skipped Ash's rehearsal dinner. But if I had, would Ash be married to an adulteress, but still speaking to me?

So, yes, at this point I'm eavesdropping, but for purely professional reasons.

"I bet you're glad you didn't set me up with her now, aren't you?" Darcy asks.

Another pause.

"I don't care how lovely of a girl she is, Mom. She pulled the pin and threw a grenade directly into her brother's lap. And I bet she was drunk when she did it. Would you really want me involved with someone that socially destructive?"

And that's the moment I realize that Darcy is talking about me. Because of course my mother's best friend was at Ash's rehearsal dinner.

It's also when Darcy notices that someone is walking behind him. He looks over his shoulder, gives me a polite, tight-lipped smile, and lowers his voice.

He hasn't lowered it enough. Or maybe trauma has given me super-hearing. But his next words are as clear as can be.

"Of course it was his fiancé's fault," Darcy says. "And the best man's. But Heather humiliated Ash in front of a room full of his closest friends on what was supposed to be the best night of his life. You can't tell me there was no other way to handle it. What kind of person does that?"

And there it is.

Ultimately, Darcy isn't my nemesis because he didn't know me. He's my nemesis because he did. He saw my actions clearly for what they were, and he held a giant mirror up in front of my face. He forced me to stare into my own selfishness and immaturity when I wanted to stay a victim.

And for that, I can never forgive him.

Chapter 9

Imposter Syndrome

I don't hear from F.W. over the weekend, but when I check email on my phone after my Syntax 1 seminar, a reply is waiting. I glance around the room to make sure its cleared out, then sit in a chair in the front row to read.

From: CR4@janereimagined.com
To: AnneElliot2024@gmail.com

Dear Ms. E.,

Well, isn't that embarrassing. Not what you wrote, but that I sent that email in the first place. I'm attempting to regret it and failing.

You normally write fantasy? If you bring the same depth to your characters in that genre, I might be tempted to step outside my comfort zone and give it a try. Is there somewhere I can read your work?

"Daddy issues" are a difficult thing. My father was present, but unavailable. I didn't play football or lacrosse or even baseball, which meant he had little use for me. I dabbled in soccer for a few years, but it didn't hold my interest. Luckily for my father, my youngest brother (there is a sister between us) fulfills all of his athletic dreams, and is

now playing lacrosse for a prestigious university on the East Coast whose name I will not drop. There shall be no humble-bragging between us.

I hope you reply, particularly if you intend to send me a fantasy writing sample.

And please, overshare to your heart's content.
F.W.

F.W. is a man. Huh.

Wait . . . Fredrick Wentworth . . . Anne Elliot's love interest. F.W. most likely isn't F.W. any more than I'm Ms. E.

But still, he's a man.

A man who likes my writing. Too bad he's into Jane Austen instead of fantasy. Not that I couldn't get over that. I mean, who doesn't like a good Austen novel?

Except, he's into Jane Austen enough to be a reader for *Jane, Reimagined.* Which means he's not casual about it.

And there's only one man . . . But, no. There is no way F.W. could be . . . &$%#!

I'm jumping to conclusions. Let's go through what I know. He definitely has a sister and a brother. And he would be shite at football. Soccer? No idea. I know next to nothing about the man except that he's frustrating and cares about his students. And about Jane Austen.

I hit reply, my thumbs swiping quickly across the screen.

From: AnneElliot2024@gmail.com
To: CR4@janereimagined.com

Dear F.W.,
Are you Darcy Delancey?

I write it. I delete it.

I write and delete it again. There is no way the universe could be this unkind.

It's not like I have any feelings whatsoever for F.W. I literally just realized he's a he. But the idea of Darcy Delancey reading my work, of finding it "heart-wrenching, insightful and provocative?"

And I have his words memorized.

Now that I think of it, it sounds like him. All pretentious. How did I miss that before? And why does it still make me feel so good?

I just won't reply. And if I end up on the short-list and he realizes who I am, there will be nothing, or at least very little, to regret.

Except . . . did I tell Darcy Delancey that I have "daddy issues"? Someone end me now.

Chapter 10

The what ifs

"It's probably not Darcy, you know."

Olivia is eating a pint of Haagan-Daz and listening to me whine. So a normal Tuesday night in the bungalow.

"What do you mean it's probably not Darcy?" I ask incredulously.

"I just mean that you could be throwing away a connection with someone who wants to read your fantasy writing and is in some way connected to the literary world on the off chance that he's secretly your nemesis. What are the chances, really?"

"Well, he's a man involved with a Jane Austen writing contest, so pretty good."

"There are lots of men who love Jane Austen."

"So you're saying he could be gay or somewhere across the Atlantic just as easily as he could be Darcy."

"Exactly. Just imagine those words he said in a British accent . . . Heart-wrenching . . . Provocative . . . What was the other?"

I sigh.

"Insightful. And your British accent needs work."

Olivia shrugs. "I'm a physicist, not a voice actor. And I'm just saying you shouldn't throw this opportunity away."

I drop my head into my hands. "He said soccer."

"What?"

"Soccer. As a separate entity from football. Baseball. No cricket. No rugby. This man is American."

"He could still be gay."

"Yes, he could still be gay. Which puts the chances of this turning into anything romantic back on par with it being Darcy."

"For someone who hates the idea of true love, you're pretty eager to see the possibilities. Or lack thereof. Let this be friendship, maybe a professional opportunity."

"I blame Jane Austen," I say. "I didn't have this problem when I was focusing on fantasy. It's all this 'who will she marry' as the major plotline that's messing with my mojo."

Olivia shrugs. "You're talking to the wrong audience. 'True love wins' books are my favorite."

"Well," I say, "this just proves it. True love can kiss my tatts."

Chapter 11

We aren't friends

"Is there a reason you're looking at me that way, Professor Higgins?"

I know I've been staring, and since I don't really care whether or not I make Darcy Delancey uncomfortable, I haven't attempted to hide it.

"Why did you buy my coffee the other day?" I ask.

He quirks his head, a little like a puppy dog attempting to figure out a math problem.

"Because it seemed like a friendly thing to do?" he asks.

"But we aren't friends," I say. He may wince, just a little. I can't tell for sure.

"We're colleagues," he says. "That should be reason enough to attempt to create a hospitable environment, shouldn't it?"

I don't reply. Just walk across the hallway to my own office and close the door.

Once I'm safely hidden away in my box, I pull up my email, the one I made for anonymity's sake when entering the *Jane, Reimagined* contest.

From: AnneElliot2024@gmail.com
To: CR4@janereimagined.com

Dear F.W.,

Are you Darcy Delancey?

It's still there, in drafts. It's been three days since F.W. wrote, and I'm starting to feel like a jerk. What if it isn't Darcy and I've ghosted the poor guy, right after he shared something personal with me.

I lower my head, pinching the bridge of my nose. I'm not that kind of person. I'm the kind on the other end, getting their feelings hurt when people realize I'm too much and drop me.

From: AnneElliot2024@gmail.com
To: CR4@janereimagined.com

Dear F.W.,

I'm sorry it's taken me so long to reply. I was in the hospital.

No

My mother was dying.

No.

I was swallowed by a dragon and just made it out the other end.

I really should be better at this. I call myself an author.

I thought you might be my secret nemesis, and I can't handle the idea that you're actually a decent human being.

Why am I not a grown-up yet?

Dear F.W.,

I'm sorry it's taken me so long to reply. I created this email exclusively for the contest, and forgot that it's not linked to the rest of my accounts.

There. That implies that I hadn't checked it, without actually lying.

I've fixed that oversight and should get any messages in a timely manner now.

If it makes you feel better, I'm lousy at sports as well. My mother signed me up for t-ball and I spent most games in right field rubbing these little flowers that smelled like pears on the underside of my nose. The only time the ball came my way, the center fielder got to it and threw it towards the infield while I waved to all my shouting and gesturing teammates.

Re. my fantasy writing, none of it has been published. I've got several polished, full-length manuscripts, but no offers of representation. Self-publishing is a valid option, but I'm not sure I'm ready to jump into all that entails. I just want to write, you know. And Carmen Alexander? She's my dream agent, and she represents across several genres.

As for you reading one, though, oh my. Do you know what a scary ask that is? Yeah, you read my Jane, Reimagined submission, but this is different. I care about fantasy.

I pause here, take a deep breath. The only people who have read my Fantasy work are online friends with zero real-life crossover potential. Not even Olivia has read it. (This is because there's no love story and I didn't want to impose it upon her, not because she's unwilling.) If there's a chance F.W. is Darcy . . . After some shifting and uncomfortable face rubbing I steal myself for war. Or, you know, to attach a document.

Here's a short story, fan fic I wrote from one of my favorite authors. If you enjoy it, you can read any of his work without going wrong, or if you ask super nicely, I just might let you try a full length of mine.

I'd love to hear what you think. Do you write yourself?

Ms. E.

I attach my short story and click send.

I'm tempted to walk across the hall and stalk Darcy to see if maybe he just got an email that's holding his interest, but I don't do it.

Tattoo 11: Sushi

Olivia and I have matching tattoos.

We got them a month after my brother's attempted wedding because Olivia, the kindest person on the planet, is constitutionally incapable of watching someone wallow without stepping in.

She said it wasn't fair that Darcy, who I hate, got a tattoo and she, who was destined to be my best friend forever, didn't. But really, she was just trying to distract me. To take my mind off of how my brother had blocked me from his phone and all his socials. How my emails went unread, and messages send through Mom were met with "He just can't talk right now, honey. Give him some time."

I think I hit all the stages of grief as I mourned the loss of my brother. And Olivia, sweet Olivia, became closer than she ever would have been had all my walls and entire life not been rubble.

She tried to convince me to get a lowercase letter phi, but I told her 1- I have no idea what that means and 2- if one of my tattoos ever makes someone think I'm in a sorority, I'm having it removed, scar tissue or no.

Now we have sushi ankle tattoos, because sushi's simple and delicious and a kind of pain I can handle.

Chapter 12
The Short List

"I made the short list!" I scream and throw my hands in the air. I'm shaking, nodding, swooping. The generous among you might say "dancing."

I run into Olivia's room and flip on the light, singing her name. She bolts upright, blonde hair mussed and eyes squinted.

"Guess what?" I say.

Olivia flops back onto her pillow.

"If this isn't better than the dream of Ryan Gosling that you just interrupted, you are in all kinds of trouble."

I pause a second to consider, but really, it's not like she can go back to it at this point.

"Better," I say. "Way better."

She closes her eyes. "You might as well tell me."

"I made the short list. In the *Jane, Reimagined* writing contest," I shriek.

"The what?"

"The *Jane, Reimagined* writing contest."

"The one that has you secretly emailing Delancey?" Olivia asks.

"You're the one who said it probably isn't him!"

"That was before you woke me up at whatever ungodly hour this is."

"Ten o'clock, Olivia. Not that ungodly."

Olivia rolls over and hugs her pillow. "I want my Ryan back."

I wait patiently. Olivia and I have been roommates long enough that I know she can't go back to sleep once she's awake, even if it's 4am. The pillow does nothing to stifle her growl as she rolls back over.

"Fine. Show me."

"Look," I say. "Right there. Third from the top." Olivia squints at my phone.

"Heather, that's not your name."

I roll my eyes, although I'm sure she can't see it around the screen I'm holding in front of her face.

"It's my pen name for this contest. Ms. Elliott."

"Not your most original," she says.

"It's the real writing that counts," I say. "And making sure that Darcy Delancey had no idea I was stepping a foot into his world, on the off chance that he's involved."

"Which I'm thinking is a better chance by the minute, with the kind of karma you're accruing," Olivia says. She's only spiteful when she's sleepy. Or hungry. She's a little bit Jekyll and Hyde, now that I think about it.

"If I get you caffeine, will you forgive me?" I ask.

"With whipped cream," she says. "From Cozie's, not the coffee factory."

Olivia has a real problem with chain coffee shops.

"Of course."

"Fine," Olivia says. "When will you find out if you won?"

I scan the email, but I already know the answer. "They're having a banquet to honor the short list and announce the grand prize winner next Saturday, September twenty-first. They'd like all nominees to attend in person if possible."

"Next Saturday? Why would they do it so soon if they wanted people to attend?" Olivia asks.

I shrug. "They mentioned the awards date in the application process. Maybe they assumed people would save it in case."

"Why is that date so familiar?" Olivia asks. She has an amazing head for numbers. It'll be dropping any second now.

"Noooooo!" Olivia says. She's snags her phone off the nightstand scowling. "It's my cousin Tanya's wedding. I'll be in Syracuse for four days."

I knew this. It's why I didn't tell her to save the date when I applied. With Olivia's parents, family is priority.

"Don't worry about it," I say, trying to head off the guilt that comes so easily for my best friend. "I'll find another plus one. Or I'll go alone. It's not a big deal."

"You should take Darcy," Olivia says. We both bust out laughing.

Chapter 13

Congratulations

From: CR4@janereimagined.com
To: AnneElliot2024@gmail.com

Dear Ms. E.

Congratulations! I'm so pleased to see that you made the short list. I'm not surprised, but honestly, in contests like these, sometimes the stories I think have the least merit end up with a champion amongst the judges and displace more worthy contenders. I'm glad that wasn't the case this time.

Don't worry about your reply taking a few days. Can you imagine if we were writing letters? I don't know if I'd have that kind of patience.

I read your fan fic, and I loved it. I wonder if I'd have loved it more or less if the true author had introduced me to the characters initially. I would guess less. Fantasy is well outside of my wheelhouse, and I doubt I'd have considered it in the first place.

You may not believe this, since we met through Jane, Reimagined, but I'm actually a political thriller guy. Maybe because the heroes' lives are so far removed from my own.

Regardless, I would love to read one of your full works, if you'd allow me that honor. And no, I'm not a writer myself.

Sincerely,

F.W.

PS- Will you be able to attend the awards ceremony? I do plan to be there.

From: AnneElliot2024@gmail.com
To: CR4@janereimagined.com
Dear F.W.,

Have you ever tried to use your thumb and forefinger to make something in real life bigger so you can see the details? I just did this with the teeny tiny directions that came with my new smoke alarm. Obviously, it did nothing but make me feel stupid. So naturally, I'm telling you all about it. If I could choose a mediocre super-power, the ability to magnify my vision might be it. I ended up taking a picture of the instructions with my phone and zooming in the old-fashioned way.

Speaking of tiny pictures, is there a story behind your profile pic being a Muppet? With your latest admission re. political thrillers, I'd expect a pic of John Hamm, or maybe Ewan McGregor. But Animal? It doesn't seem to fit what yo've shared so far.

I've attached an epub of my favorite, many-times-rejected novel, The Winter Mist. You can transfer it to Kindle and read to your heart's content. Meanwhile, I shall distract myself with my real life and await your verdict.

Ms. E.

PS- I will be attending the awards ceremony.

Tattoo 12: The Betta Fish

From: CR4@janereimagined.com

To: AnneElliot2024@gmail.com

Dear Ms. E.,

The picture you reference is actually not Animal, which would have been an odd choice indeed, but is a betta fish. The picture was chosen for me by an 83 year old woman with a golden heart who told me she did so in deference to my hair, "so lovely and wavy." I believe she's approaching dementia, but as I don't make it a habit to argue with the elderly, I let it be. It is just a fish, after all. If you could abstain from beta male jokes, it would be appreciated.

I will not write more at the moment. I have a manuscript to read . . .

F.W.

PS- Will you be bringing a plus one?

I stare, dumbfounded. There is so much here that I don't even know where to start.

It looks innocuous, right? A betta fish and an old lady liking his hair.

But I have an absolutely enormous Betta Fish tattoo. It stretches from my shoulder to my elbow in rainbow colored glory. And to omit such a thing from this conversation seems almost sacrilegious, especially since I will be meeting this person at the awards ceremony and my intended dress is a sleeveless black sheath. He will find it odd I didn't mention it, or, if he's secretly a narcissist, he may even think I got it for him.

Fine. I know that's ridiculous. But my brain isn't working well right now, because Darcy Delancey's hair is lovely and wavy, and because this mysterious pen pal, who may or may not be him, just asked if I'm bringing a plus one.

Normally, this would be such an easy question to answer. Olivia has been my plus one for the last five years. But Olivia will be across the country at her cousin Tanya's wedding, and I've already hit my lifelong quota in the ruining weddings department.

Who else can I bring? My mom? I mean, she'd come, if I ask. As long as she doesn't have something already on her calendar, which honestly at this point is a long shot. With all of her charity auctions and art openings and what not it's amazing she's ever available.

But surely F.W. is fishing (no pun intended) to see if I have a boyfriend, right? Which is lamer? Saying I'm coming to an awards dinner alone, or that I'm bringing my mother . . .

I drop my head to my desk hoping for inspiration.

And in case you're wondering, the Betta on my arm was in celebration of tattoo parlors opening back up after Covid. Being told I couldn't for months made me want a tattoo that much more. Beyond that, it had no other story. Until now.

Chapter 14

Maybe it's Carmen Alexander?

"Maybe it's Carmen Alexander," Olivia says out of nowhere.

We've been lounging/reading/scrolling in the bungalow's tiny backyard for about half an hour. Really, doing all we can to soak up the September warmth before October is upon us with all its unpredictability.

I feel the need to clarify "backyard" so you don't get the wrong impression. We live walking distance (on a good, athletic day) to our urban university and have professor's salaries. Olivia's parents purchased this house so we could rent it from them, and I'm grateful. I also am choosing not to be bitter that my step-dad, who could have bought me something three times the size without batting an eye, didn't.

The "backyard" is a wooden platform on top of a concrete slab surrounded by a wooden privacy fence. Our cars are parked, single file, on the concrete, and Olivia, who is masterful with diy projects of all types, has created a screen about four feet high with plants growing on it between us and the cars. She's also put potted plants all around. We lay on the two lounge chairs, and there's a bistro table with two normal chairs off to one side.

Because Olivia is all about repurposing, and because we're generally broke, nearly everything in the space is either thrift store or found free by the road.

OK, back to Olivia's random comment.

"Maybe who's Carmen Alexander?" I ask.

"Your pen pal." My pen pal?

"Why would you say that?" I ask.

"You did send him a manuscript. Maybe your dream agent is already a big fan and this contest is now a formality."

"That's not how the universe works for me," I say.

Olivia sits up, putting her brightly colored novel on the ground beside her.

"Maybe that's because you've been reading and writing the wrong books for so long," she says, as though this is an actual possibility. "Your heroes are all struggle and toil and self-sufficiency. Maybe by writing your characters into so many tragic places you've karmically cursed yourself, but now that you've written a redemptive love story your whole narrative is changing."

I love Olivia more than I love my appendix, but sometimes that physics professor brain of hers teams up with her overindulgence in romance novels to come up with some really wacky stuff. I once asked her if she was on drugs and she was mortally offended, but it's hard to imagine someone coming up with this kind of theory without the aid of chemicals. I'm not even going to touch it.

"I'm pretty sure Carmen Alexander is a woman," I say instead.

"Pretty sure or completely certain?" Olivia asks.

"Ninety-nine percent sure," I say.

"Hmmmm. Let's ask google."

Oddly enough, for someone with a reputation like the Queenmaker's, there really aren't any photos of Carmen Alexander. Like, none. No recorded interviews, and the profile pics are always of books . . .

I finally find a fifteen year old photo of Carmen with her, that's right, her, first major client when they sold film rights to a giant studio. Carmen looks like a midwestern mom beside the actress who would go on to play the iconic "Santa Marta." The photo is in a "hot and not" segment of a celebrity magazine, and if my looks were getting torn down the way they're ripping into poor Carmen, I'd scrub the internet of my picture too.

It's not like she's ugly. She's just normal, like the rest of us. And she's definitely not a man.

"It's not Carmen Alexander," I tell Olivia. "She's a she."

"Then I have no answers for you," Olivia says and picks up her book.

Chapter 15

Plus Two, Minus one

From: AnneElliot2024@gmail.com
  To: CR4@janereimagined.com
  Dear F.W.,
  Are you Darcy Delancey?
  One of these days I'll just send it. Maybe. But not today.
  Dear F.W.,

  I see it now, the Betta Fish. I probably should have seen it before, as I have a tattoo of a Betta on my left arm. (In case you're wondering, there are no tattoos of Animal anywhere on my body.)

  I tell you this as it will be one way you can recognize me at the awards ceremony. I do not currently have a plus one. My best friend will be out of town, and while I was considering bringing a colleague, I've yet to decide. No one in my department is aware that I write fiction, let alone that I've ventured into this genre. I'm not sure anyone would believe it.

  Are you bringing a plus one?
  Ms. E.

From: CR4@janereimagined.com

To: AnneElliot2024@gmail.com

Dear Ms. E.,

When I first asked, I didn't have a plus one; however, I have since learned that my mother will be flying to town to visit with an old college friend. The only night she has open is the night of the awards, which means my mother will now be my plus one.

This is the point where I sigh and freely hand over my man card. All my attempts to impress you with my sports acumen and other accomplishments will be wiped away by the fact that I am, indeed, bringing my mother to the party.

I was hoping that we could meet at the ceremony. I would still like to do so, if you're willing. But be warned, Mrs. Bennett had nothing on my mother. In a glorious modern reversal, worthy of Jane, Reimagined itself, it's her single, just turned thirty year old son who must be married off.

F.W.

PS- I've always admired people with tattoos. It's not just the beauty of the artwork that appeals, but also the ability to commit, the decisiveness required to say "I will live with this for the rest of my life and love it always" that seems admirable to me in a way that the temporary nature of our culture seldom provides. That said, I have a small confession to make. I am tragically afraid of needles . . .

That seals it.

F.W. is Darcy Delancey.

I would have known that he recently turned thirty even without our family history because Olivia's lab nemesis, Andrew Chu, told Olivia who told me that a bunch of professors would be getting together at Fiona's to celebrate with drinks. Obviously, Olivia and I had something else to do that night.

But to the point, Darcy is thirty. F.W. is thirty. And even more to the point, Darcy would be a total wuss about needles.

I decide to text my mom to confirm.

> **Is Camilla Delancey coming to town this weekend?**

> **The prodigal daughter, and with such an oddly specific question. Yes she is. Did Darcy tell you?**

Probably. Darcy probably told me. And surely with the Betta Fish comment he knows who I am as well.

> **I'm on the short list for a writing contest, and she's going to attend with Darcy, who's part of the screening process. Do you want to be my plus one?**

> **A writing contest? Why didn't you tell me you'd won a writing contest?**

I grimace. Why didn't I tell my mother, who once called my dreams to become a fantasy author "adorable," that I was short-listed for a Jane Austen writing contest? Gee, I wonder.

> I guess it didn't come up. Plus, I haven't won. I'm just on the short list.

> It doesn't seem like you should be allowed to win a contest when you know one of the judges. Is that normal?

My mother reads my texts as well as she listens when I speak.

> He wasn't a judge. And I was anonymous.

> Of course, dear. That makes sense. I'd love to be your plus one. Where's Olivia?

> Wedding, out of town.

I can hear her sniff in my mind.

> Well, darling, I'm always here for you.

And scene.

Chapter 16

Do you know who I am?

"Do you know who I am?" I ask from the doorway of Darcy's office.

He looks up from his neat, nearly minimalistic desk, and I wonder, not for the first time, if he'd notice were I to move the framed photo of his family vacationing on the outer banks two inches to the left. Behind me a murder light flickers in the hallway.

"Do I know who you are?" he asks back.

I narrow my eyes.

"Yes?" he says, definitely a question.

"Is that why you bought me coffee?" I ask.

Darcy takes in a deep breath through his nose before replying

"Are you asking about when I bought you coffee several weeks ago?"

He's leaning forward on his elbows now, and I'm not sure if it's because he's engaged in the conversation or if he's attempting to protect his vulnerable underbelly.

"You haven't bought me coffee since," I say, shifting my bag on my shoulder.

"Do you want me to buy you coffee?" Darcy asks.

"No, I don't want you to buy me coffee. I can buy my own coffee. I just want you to tell me when you realized I'm Ms. E."

I also want him to tell me if he knows I'm my mother's daughter, but I won't ask that.

"Had you even submitted your story when I bought you coffee?"

I can't remember, which is ultra-frustrating. I think I growl. I must do something startling because Darcy's eyebrows shoot for the ceiling.

"I didn't know it was you until the Betta fish tattoo," he says. "It's a bit of a giveaway."

Just like I knew it would be. But then he said he admires people with tattoos . . . And he said so many nice things about my writing, before he knew he was saying those things to me. Whatever. I'm not out to impress Darcy Delancey.

"So what do we do now?" I ask.

That stupid puppy solving math problems look is back on his face.

I don't want to give you the impression Darcy always looks confused. Most of the time he looks like he's humoring me, or secretly laughing at me. Or maybe like he's thinking about something completely unrelated and pretending to listen.

"How about," he says "we stop pretending that we have nothing in common and actually be friends?"

I tilt my head. I bet now I'm the one who looks confused.

"Do you know who my mom is?" I ask.

"Should I?"

So typical. Smugly thinking he knows the whole story. He will, though.

"I'm going to bring my mom to the awards ceremony too," I say. "Won't that be fun?"

"I'm sure our mothers will get along swimmingly."

Oh, Darcy, you have no idea.

"Better hold on to your pillow," I fire back, one last shot as I retreat across the hall.

Chapter 17

Reservations for four

> I've talked with Camilla, and we're all going out to dinner before the ceremony.

> Mom, it's an awards dinner. They're serving food there.

> Yes, but you never know what they'll be serving, and Camilla is on some kind of special diet again.

Darcy's mother's eating habits are legend at our house. Whether it's throwbacks like the cabbage soup or grapefruit diet or that cleanse involving cayenne pepper and maple syrup, Camilla Delancey has done it. While I've only seen her in pictures, she's never looked overweight.

> Heather, are you there?

> **Yeah**

> **We're thinking Bristol. I'll pick you up at 5:15.**

Am I really willing to enter this night without my own car? My desire not to drive downtown and the availability of Uber makes this an easy answer.

> **Me: I'll see you then.**

Should I tell her Darcy still doesn't know who I am, in relationship to him and his past? It's shocking that his mom has never mentioned it. But maybe not so shocking, since this is Camilla.

We'll just let everyone be surprised.

Chapter 18

Living that champagne life

Darcy rises as the hostess leads us towards their table.

"Hold onto my pillow?" he asks. "Seriously?"

The look on his face is all I could have hoped for.

"Camilla," my mom says as she bends down to air kiss her best friend's cheek. "You look lovely."

"As do you, darling," Camilla says. She's remained seated and is now reaching for a glass of something sparkling before her.

I take my seat and Darcy pushes it in behind me. What the?

"Isn't this lovely?" Camilla asks. "The four of us together. And to think you've been colleagues this whole time and never known the connection."

I force a tight smile Darcy's way.

"Oh, Heather knew," my mother says. "I told her before they started, and it's not like Delancey is a common name."

"That is interesting, isn't it?" Darcy asks. "Heather, how is it that you never mentioned the connection? And you have a different name than your mother. Oh, wait."

I can see him assembling the pieces. My father's death, that I told him about in the email. The wedding we were in together as children.

"She uses her birth father's name," my mother supplies with a tight smile, "despite being legally adopted shortly after I remarried."

"Daddy issues," I say, my mother's same forced smile now on my lips.

Camilla laughs like I've said something delightful, and I wonder what's in her glass and how many she's had.

"My mother is on the champagne diet," Darcy says, answering my unspoken thoughts.

"I see."

There's a moment of silence at the table, and we're rescued by a waiter arriving with our drinks and an appetizer that Darcy must have ordered before we arrived. After our orders are taken, the mothers begin chattering as though they haven't seen each other for the last several days already. Darcy takes the opportunity to speak low, for my ears only.

"You never thought it worth mentioning that your mother is Brenda Randolf?"

"I did, once, but you were invested in a conversation with the dean and unable to break away." Or make room. "I suppose the opportunity didn't arise after that."

I can tell he wants to ask what in the world I'm talking about, but at that moment his mother spills champagne across her empty bread plate, and Darcy is too busy making sure it doesn't get onto her clothing before the waiter can make it back to our table to assist.

The rest of the meal proceeds without incident, and we take separate cars to the awards venue. To be fair to my mother, the food served there isn't nearly as good as what we had at Bristol. There is no champagne in sight, not even when the winner is announced.

Tattoo 7: The Queen's Crown

I'm a little bit embarrassed about this one. And remember, I was not embarrassed to tell you I have a raccoon on my butt. So please, be kind.

I mentioned that Carmen Alexander is my dream agent. She has been for always, ever since I realized who an agent was and what they do.

Carmen Alexander is "the Queenmaker." One very intoxicated night, after yet another query was "closed due to no response," I decided I didn't need anyone else to declare me a queen, thank you very much. In a burst of self-righteous, feminist defiance that would have made the early suffragettes proud (maybe), I took an Uber to the tattoo parlor and crowned myself.

Pain is a stimulant. Did you know that? So I was all alertness as the crown was tattooed very (very) low on my stomach. So low you don't even see it when I'm in a modest bikini.

It's been good birth control, really. The few times I've considered letting a man see me naked, I've asked myself "how will he respond to my crown?" None of their imaginary responses has merited a reveal.

Chapter 19

Jealousy

Darcy and his mother have been a wonderful distraction so far this evening, but as I enter the lobby of the prestigious downtown hotel that's hosting the *Jane, Reimagined* awards ceremony, I feel the butterflies in my stomach revive.

I'm glad my mother is my plus one. She's in her element as we walk through the lobby to the small ballroom where the ceremony will be held. I'm not sure what I was expecting. Maybe wait staff in period attire, or at the least a slide show of "best ever" Jane Austen adaptations playing on the enormous tv screen at the back of the room. There's none of that. In fact, if there wasn't a sign by the door reading *"Jane, Reimagined* awards celebration" in an elegant, old-worldly font, I would have thought I'd been tricked into attending the annual end-of-year professor's meet and greet.

I tell myself that a fantasy awards presentation wouldn't take place in a castle or forest. That the servers wouldn't be wearing elven ears or fairy wings. But still, I'm just a little underwhelmed.

That is, until I see her. Carmen Alexander is here.

I'm glad I googled her picture, because there is nothing to make her stand out from the crowd. No spotlight rains down upon her black pants suit, chunky necklace and sensible flats. It's like looking at Strider in the taproom of the Prancing Pony and knowing that the glory of Aragorn, son of Arathorn, Isildur's heir lies hidden beneath his worn travelers garb. Or for those of you who are more super-hero inclined (read: genre-deprived), it's the unassuming Peter Parker before he dons his Spidey-suit.

Before I can make a fool of myself and fan-girl all over her, Darcy approaches. Not me. Her.

Darcy reaches out and casually draws Carmen into a one-armed hug. A hug? I've never seen Darcy hug anyone besides his own mother, and now his arm is around Carmen Alexander. He says something as he releases her, and it must be charming because she laughs and swats at Darcy with her little purse.

Am I jealous of the fifty-something year old woman laughing with Darcy Delancey? Heck no! Am I jealous of Darcy Delancey, being all besties with the agent of my dreams?

Yes. Yes I am.

Darcy must feel my dagger eyes scorching his perfect face because he looks my direction. And then he does the unthinkable.

Darcy Delancey lifts his chin in acknowledgement.

Oh, I want to punch him. If he had a pillow, I'd throw it across the room.

Am I over-reacting to a minor gesture? Yes, I can admit that.

But that chin lift, directed by overly-confident, self-satisfied males, has been pissing me off for two decades now. And Darcy Delancey has managed to make it worse with that gorgeous hair of his. I swear, if you'd asked me before this moment if that kind of flopping and flowing could be achieved without special effects and fans and a slow motion camera, I'd have said no way. But there it is.

Carmen looks my way and smiles, brows lowering slightly. Oh, crap. Am I scowling? I force thoughts of Darcy's hair from my mind and paste on a smile.

Darcy motions with his hand, waving me over. The anticipation I've been feeling over the prospect of meeting Carmen Alexander clashes with the years of latent hostility towards Darcy. But this, this right now, is his redemption. He is forgiven all.

I can feel the crowd parting before me, feel those cameras panning in on this moment of destiny. Screw *Jane, Reimagined*. This is why I wrote that story in the first place. This is why I'm here. The culmination of years of writing and submitting and teaching college students with their naivety and sparkling hope just to pay the bills. All for this moment . . .

I've taken only three steps when a horrible screeching fills the air. It's followed by an embarrassed chuckle and a woman's nasal voice.

"Sorry about that," the voice says. "Oh, technology."

My gaze shifts towards the podium at the front of the room where a petite, silver-haired woman with a broach the size of a lemon at her throat smiles nervously. She chuckles again, this time joined by the polite crowd.

"Please, we need everyone to find their seats," she says. "We have a schedule to keep, but there will be plenty of time to chat and mingle after the meal."

No. This can't be happening. Not when I'm this close.

I look back towards Darcy who meets my eyes and shrugs. Carmen touches his arm and inclines her head towards her table. Darcy nods.

And it's over. My chance is gone.

I feel that familiar sinking in my gut, the one that comes fresh with every form rejection email. But no. This opportunity isn't gone. It's just postponed. With a deep breath, I cling to the announcer's promise that there will be more time to mingle after dinner. Surely Darcy can introduce me then.

My mother, oblivious to my inner turmoil, threads her hand through my elbow.

"We're over here, darling," she says. "I took the liberty of asking a host while you were staring at Darcy."

"I wasn't staring at Darcy," I say on reflex. And I wasn't. That was a simple trick of proximity. A memory of his hair falling back into place calls me on my lie, but I can honestly say that Darcy was NOT the main attraction. There's no way I'll be able to convince my mother of this, so I don't bother trying.

My mother leads me to our table, and I sit at the hand-written place card labeled "Heather Higgins, aka Ms. E.; *Persuaded*." I'm glad to be in one of the forward-facing seats, as the middle-aged couple across from me has no view but our table and the doors that exit into the hall.

I, on the other hand, from my seat at the very, very back, can see the whole room. Carmen Alexander sits right up front, chatting animatedly with the young woman to her right. Darcy and his mother are at the next table over. Between us is a chasm filled with grey hair and black dinner jackets. For the first time I wonder if my placement means

I didn't win. Not that I care if I win, per say, but Carmen . . . I take yet another deep breath, reminding myself that this is not Jane Austen's era. I don't need to concern myself with my status amongst this very limited society in order to fulfill any viable path to a comfortable future. I am a queen in my own right, and this isn't even my genre.

"These centerpieces are so unique, aren't they Heather?" my mother says from my elbow. I'm sure she's never been this far back in a room in her life, but I appreciate the brave face she's putting on. And she's doing it for me, to support me. My chest warms, despite the air conditioning vent directly overhead.

"They are unique, aren't they?" I agree. Made up of antique-looking Jane Austen novels and a small container of flowers, the centerpieces are a nice touch.

"I wonder if any of them are first editions," the woman to my left says.

In Austen's day, being seated between two women would have been a terrible embarrassment that emphasized my spinster status. But this is not the 1800's, and in our glorious modern age it means nothing except that I chose my mother as my plus one. Which is not a shout-out to my spinster status. Shut up.

"I bet they keep the first editions closer to the stage," the woman's companion says. He's a man roughly her age with a full head of russet hair that may or may not be original to his head.

"We did seem to end up in the cheap seats, didn't we?" the woman asks, and giggles. The look they share makes me think that they'd be just as happy at McDonalds, as long as they were together.

My traitorous eyes glance towards Darcy's table, but he isn't there. Instead, he's ten feet from us and closing, Camilla gliding beside him.

Chapter 20

Upgrade

"I did warn you that my mother is a bit like Mrs. Bennett, didn't I?" Darcy asks.

My hand is cradled in his elbow as he leads me towards the front of the room. His words are spoken low, mouth tilted so close to my ear that I feel as much as hear them. My shiver is involuntary.

Of course Camilla couldn't sit at such a prestigious table and eat nothing. It would be gauche. And besides, she so rarely got to see her oldest and dearest friend. It was cruel to put them in the same room and separate them. Surely Heather could understand . . .

Darcy doesn't seem nearly as bothered as he should be by the obvious and premeditated matchmaking ploy. He nods and smiles to pearl-wearing septuagenarians as we weave our way past seated guests. I endure the quizzical gazes, viscerally aware that there isn't another visible tattoo in the room.

When we reach my new table, Darcy introduces me to the group as a whole. "Heather Higgins, a dear family friend, as well as a short list recipient."

There are smiles and nods all around, and then the group goes back to their own conversations. I now have a man on both sides. Lucky me. The man on my left is a stout gentleman with no facial hair and what I first believe to be a napkin in his collar but then realize is an actual cravat. He's tucked into his chicken with abandon.

I'm not surprised to see that the books on this table arrangement do seem a bit more impressive.

"So this is how the other half lives, huh Darcy?" I ask.

His smile holds a question.

"The other half?"

"You know, the upper class of Austenism. The elite of the ton."

"Ah, I see," he says with a humoring smile. He glances towards the centerpiece. "No second editions for our table."

I can't help but smile at how well he reads me. No pun intended.

"You know, Heather, you were born into the same world I was."

I force my smile to remain as I nod to the waiter who's offering to fill my wine glass. "Blue blood by birth, or half blue anyway," I say. "Outcast by choice."

It's not exactly true. I never fit in, even when I was still trying. But that isn't a conversation I need to have with Darcy. I reach for my wine and take a sip. It's mid, but you know what they say about beggars.

Darcy looks like he's about to reply, but he changes his mind and takes a sip of his own wine. I laugh when he grimaces.

"Not quite what you're used to, Fitzwilliam?" I ask.

"It's quite nice," he lies.

I spend the next several minutes moving the vegetables around on my plate while Darcy chats with the woman on his right. My stomach is churning with nerves, and by the time the waiters are delivering dessert, I realize that a trip to the ladies is in order. Before I can excuse myself, the woman seated across the table from me rises and makes her way to the podium. Unsurprisingly, it's the same voice as before.

I won't bore you with details. Just know that the long list of people being acknowledged, including both Darcy Delancey and Carmen Alexander in their turns, is barely enough to distract me from the roiling in my gut.

Then it comes.

The big reveal.

The reason we're here.

The winner of this year's *Jane, Reimagined* short story contest and the one on one with Carmen Alexander is . . . not me.

Not anyone I know, which, really, would only have been that sweet couple I met back in the cheap seats.

Coincidentally or not, the winner is a lovely young woman in a rust orange slip dress who was already seated directly beside Carmen Alexander. The two hug before the young woman advances to the stage to claim her award.

Darcy leans close, so only I can hear.

"I preferred your story," he says with a small smile.

I give him a nod. It was kindly meant.

As soon as the presentation wraps, I make my way to the ladies room to take care of long-overdue business. And maybe to compose myself, just a little. Because it's been a while since I let myself want something as much as I wanted that one on one. But it's fine.

I'm only gone a couple of minutes, but when I return to the ballroom, Carmen is gone. Darcy stands with our mothers near the front of the room congratulating the night's winner. She's younger than most of the people here, possibly even younger than I am. Her hair is shiny, and as I get close I realize her nails perfectly match the dress. I glance at my own bare nails and curl them into a protective fist at my side.

I join the circle in time to hear Camilla say "You have a bright future ahead of you now, Ms. Cadera. My son is in the field already. I'm sure he could give you some tips if you're interested in getting coffee with him."

I snort and attempt to cover with a cough, but I don't think anyone buys it. My smirk doesn't help.

Darcy's smile is the polite version he normally saves for staff meetings when the dean is particularly unreasonable.

"Actually," Darcy says, reaching out and drawing me against his side, "Heather and I would be happy to meet with you, wouldn't we Heather?" He's smiling down at me like I'm the prettiest thing in the room, but his eyes dare me to call him on his lie. I would, if it was only Darcy who'd be embarrassed, but a quick glance shows me Ms. Cadera's discomfort. I'm not petty enough to ruin her big night.

"Of course we would," I say, reaching my arm around Darcy's waist and pinching him on the side where no one can see. There is no give. Is this man doing sit-ups in his office when the door's closed?

"I'm ok, really," Ms. Cadera says. "I'm sure Carmen can handle my career from here."

There's nothing in her voice or expression to indicate cattiness, but it still hurts. Darcy squeezes me just a little tighter.

"I'm sure she can," he says. "It was a pleasure to meet you, and again, congratulations."

For a moment I'm grateful for Darcy's arm around my shoulder. Sure, Ms. Cadera won the contest, but I got the man. Or at least the appearance of it.

Wait. Did my brain just think that? That's it. I'm off regency romance forever.

I casually step away from Darcy, but not before I see the look that passes between our mothers. This will not end well.

Chapter 21

Rideshare

My body is tense as I squint through the river pouring down my windshield. The wipers' swish is frantic, but ineffective, and the extra time I gave myself has been eaten up by the rain. I hope Olivia isn't too hangry after her flight.

I enter the arrivals tunnel at the newly built Kansas City airport just as my phone pings. Pulling to the side, I turn off my wipers and read the text from Olivia.

`By column 1G.`

Merging back into traffic, I drive until I see her. She's right where she said, but she's talking to a man. I can only see his back. He's tall, dark hair . . . No way.

The man who turns and scans the cars is Andrew Chu, Olivia's in-lab nemesis. The one she blames for catching her hair on fire. Or, in acid, anyway.

Olivia waves at me, and I pull to the curb beside them and roll down my window.

"Thank God," Olivia says, poking her head into the car. "Did you bring snacks?"

"Of course I did," I say, smiling. I look past her at Andrew. "Did you pick up a stray? What's with Chu?"

Olivia rolls her eyes then says in a sweet voice "I did. He followed me all the way back from Boston."

Andrew bumps up alongside Olivia and grins into my car.

"Good evening, Heather. It's a wet one, yeah?"

His shoulder is almost touching Olivia's, and she isn't cringing away. Before I can answer his inane comment about the weather, Olivia pipes in.

"Can we drop him off at his place? I already said yes, but you could always say no."

I snort. "You're coming with us, Andrew." I pop the trunk, and Andrew grabs both his own and Olivia's suitcase and carries them to the foot of the car.

His enthusiasm for a car ride reminds me of the pug I had when I was little. Not that anything else about Andrew is pug-ish. In fact, if Olivia didn't hate him so much, I'd even say he's attractive. In a non-threatening, boy-band way.

Olivia opens the door and collapses into the passenger seat.

"Snacks," she says.

"Glovebox. And what's going on?"

Before she can answer, Andrew opens the rear passenger door. He folds his long legs into the back seat like this isn't weird at all.

"The rain was really coming down when we landed," Andrew says. His obsession with the weather would have fit him right into an Austen novel.

"Yeah, hasn't let up," I agree, pulling back into traffic.

Olivia's mouth is filled with a trail mix bar, but she gestures behind us with the Twizzler bag, clearly offering one to Andrew. I bite the inside of my cheek to make sure I'm not dreaming. Olivia does not share candy after a flight.

"No thanks," Andrew says. "I'm just grateful for the ride. Not sure many Ubers are out tonight."

Olivia has finally swallowed. "He doesn't have any friends," she says as the first sheets of water hit us.

This comment is completely on brand for Olivia with Andrew, and I probably wouldn't have noticed it on any other night. It certainly wouldn't have bothered me. Now, though, I'm wondering if this is how I sound around Darcy.

I can't see Andrew's face without taking my eyes off the road, which I won't do in this storm, but that couldn't have felt great. My mind flashes to me in Darcy's office, telling him we aren't friends.

From the back seat Andrew says, "Believe it or not, I'm generally well-liked."

"There's a difference. Heather may not be 'generally well liked,'" Olivia replies, making air quotes while holding a Twizzler in each hand, "but she has me forever."

I'm only half listening as I concentrate on not hydroplaning, but that was not a compliment. Olivia loses her sunshine when she's hungry. Andrew comes to my defense.

"Heather is well-respected," he says. "She's tough, but fair, at least by reputation."

"Heather is everything good in this world," Olivia says, doubling down and way over-shooting the truth. "She just comes off a little harsh sometimes."

"I'm here, you know," I say. "I can hear you talking about me even while I keep us all from dying in a watery grave."

"OK, pot," Andrew says.

"What?" from Olivia.

I'm confused too. Did he just call me pot?

"You said Heather comes off harsh? That's the pot calling the kettle black."

Ah. I'm not actually here after all. Andrew is definitely still talking to Olivia.

"What are you, eighty years old? Who says that?" Olivia asks.

Andrew mumbles something that sounds like "point proven," and then there's silence.

"Olivia, find us music," I say.

By the time we reach Andrew's apartment the storm outside my car has let up. Inside the atmosphere is all silent tension emphasized occasionally by the crescendo of a Mozart sonata.

"Thanks for the ride," Andrew tells me as I pull into a loading space in front of his apartment building.

"Anytime," I say.

He gets out and grabs his suitcase from the trunk then stands beside the passenger door. Olivia stares straight ahead. I put down her window (the power of the driver's seat) and lean forward so I can see him around her profile.

"Good to see you, Andrew," I say. He nods, glances at Olivia again, and then straightens his shoulders and turns for his building.

I put up the window and direct the car towards home.

"Andrew Chu, huh?" I ask. "How'd that happen?"

"He was at the wedding," Olivia says. "Friends with the groom."

I wait for more, but she doesn't give it.

"For a minute it seemed like you didn't hate him," I say.

"Yeah," she agrees. "Apparently I only hate him in Kansas City."

"Inconvenient, that," I say.

"Yep," she agrees. "Let's make milkshakes."

"Works for me."

We're drinking chocolate shakes and Olivia is telling me about her cousin's wedding, after hearing all about my Darcy drama, when my phone pings. It's my mom.

> **Do you have plans Wednesday evening? If not, save it for me.**

Well that's sweet. It's been a minute since my mother wanted to hang out for no reason.

> **You've got it. What are we doing?**

> **I'll pick you up at 6:00. Dress nice.**

The fact that she didn't answer my question is not lost on me, but I'm more interested in how Olivia no longer seems to spit out Andrew's name like a nut gone rancid. One mystery at a time.

Chapter 22

I could have lied.

"Good afternoon, Professor Higgins."

I look up from my desk Monday afternoon to see Darcy in the doorway. He's holding two cups and a paper bag I recognize from the Cranky Bean.

"May I?" He edges into my office and puts a cup and the bag on my desk.

"What's this for?" I ask.

"Isn't this what a fake boyfriend does? Bring coffee?"

I pick up the coffee. "You are not my fake boyfriend," I say. "And you're interfering with my nap schedule." I take a sip of pistachio latte, closing my eyes as the heavenly sweetness rolls over my tongue. Oh, I would give up a nap for this . . .

"About that," Darcy says.

"About what?"

Darcy glances at the chair before my desk like he's considering using it. Lucky for me, it's already occupied by a stack of books and my tennis shoes. He leans awkwardly against the doorjamb then straightens again.

"My mother extended her trip. She doesn't leave until Thursday now," he says.

"And this affects me because . . . ?"

Darcy rubs the back of his neck. I'd be enjoying his discomfort were it not for the cold weight settling in my gut.

"Well, after our," Darcy pauses, grimacing, "show of affection on Saturday night, she would love for the four of us to have dinner again before she goes."

"It's already arranged with my mother, isn't it?" I ask.

"Yes."

"Wednesday night?"

He nods. I consider throwing my coffee in the trash can in protest, but really, that would just be punishing myself.

"Why did you do that, anyway?" I ask, anxiety making my voice harsher than intended.

"Is panic a valid answer?"

"No. It's not."

Darcy sighs. "I felt bad for that poor girl who'd just won the contest."

"Oh, yes. Poor girl. Just won a one on one with Carmen Alexander. She deserves all our sympathy."

The look he gives makes it clear he finds the comment beneath me.

"Fine," I say. "So you did it for the same reason I went along with it. And now Karma is biting us in the slacks for our good deed."

Darcy smirks. "It's not the worst thing that could happen," he says.

I roll my eyes. "I'll get the details from my mom. And by the way, when she asked about it in the car, I told her it was nothing."

"Of course," Darcy says.

He's nearly out the door when I remember my manners.

"Thank you," I tell his retreating back. "For the coffee."

"You're welcome," he says, smiling and making me realize how seldom, in all the Darcy smiles in my mental catalogue, I see teeth. But there they are, white and shiny with one slightly turned incisor making them perfectly imperfect.

How annoying.

When I glance from his mouth back to his eyes, one eyebrow is quirked.

"Go away," I say.

He does as he's told.

A couple of minutes later, I'm still relishing the taste of my latte, when an email comes through.

From: CR4@janereimagined.com
To: AnneElliot2024@gmail.com

Dear Ms. E., aka Heather,

I thought of lying when you confronted me about being F.W, but, at the risk of sounding way too much like my namesake, "disguise of every sort is my abhorrence."

OK, maybe that's taking it a bit far, particularly considering that I just roped you into faking a relationship we don't have. The irony is not lost on me. But I did consider canceling my plans to attend the ceremony with my mother so I could keep our conversation going. Since I chose the more straightforward path, I'm just going to ask.

Why do you hate me? I've been trying to piece it together, with all this new information I now have about your identity, but I still can't figure it out. Surely it's not the flower basket?

Any enlightenment you can give would be appreciated.

D.D.

From: AnneElliot2024@gmail.com
To: CR4@janereimagined.com

Darcy,

I don't hate you. I just don't like you. Not everyone has to, you know.

My mind flashes to Olivia and Andrew in the car last night. Am I really this mean to him normally? I cringe, remembering not long ago when I blatantly, and with a smile, told Darcy that we aren't friends.

Fine. Let's try this again, but with less attitude. Channel my inner Ms. E. I take a long sip of my latte for inspiration and start over.

From: AnneElliot2024@gmail.com
To: CR4@janereimagined.com

Darcy,

I don't hate you. I was in a really bad place when we first met, and hoping you could be an ally in a new environment. Instead, you boxed me out of your conversation with the dean, and then I overheard you condemning me to your mother over how I handled my brother's rehearsal dinner. (In case you were wondering, my brother still isn't talking to me, and my step-father is more distant than ever.)

I now know that I was a complete stranger you were ignoring at the new hire function, and I won't attempt to argue that I handled my brother's situation well. That said, it's rude to see a stranger at an event like that and turn your back rather than inviting her into the circle. You basically gave me the cut direct. And then how you were blasting me, to your mother, no less . . . Elitist. Judgmental. Arrogant. You were exactly what I would have expected the boy who stole my flower basket to become.

Crap. This version is even worse. I've gone from snarky passive aggression to full-on wound exposure and lashing out. I lean forward, head between my elbows, and groan. What am I doing? And why am I not an adult yet? Aren't adults supposed to be able to handle their emotions?

Taking a deep breath, I sit up straight and look back to the screen. Time to try this again.

But . . . no. Just no . . .

It's sent.

How did that happen?

I frantically try to "unsend," but to no avail. I bolt from my chair, throw open my door and cross the hallway.

Darcy squints toward his screen, mouth turned down, shoulders drooping. Raising his eyes to meet mine, he forces his lips to turn up just a little on one side.

"That explains it, then," he says.

"Darcy, that wasn't supposed to send."

"I see." He takes a deep breath. "But, it's how you really feel. And now I know."

"It's not how I feel," I protest. "I was processing. Nothing I said in that email was fair. It's all filtered through how awful that time was."

Darcy winces, then nods, mouth pinched.

"It's fine," he says, closing the laptop and stashing it in his leather messenger bag. "I can honestly say I don't remember either interaction, but I'm genuinely sorry that I was so inconsiderate and oblivious when you needed a friend. You have my sincere apology."

He looks up, and the direct eye contact is worse than avoidance. Life was easier before I acknowledged that Darcy Delancey has feelings.

Darcy is standing now and walking towards me. What's he going to do, try to hug it out?

When he's directly before me, my hand lifts. It lands on his abdomen, below the ribs. I stare down at my perfidious fingertips, then back up in time to see Darcy shift his gaze away from mine. He clears his throat and gives a nod towards the doorway I'm blocking.

"*Intro to Georgian Lit.* seminar to get to," he says with a forced, polite smile.

I wrench my hand away like I've touched something hot. And to be fair . . . Not the time, Heather. And when did I start thinking that? Ew.

I step backwards into the hallway.

Darcy closes and locks his door behind us. He's nearly to the elevator when I call his name.

"Darcy," I say. Yell, really, down the hall. "I'm sorry."

"No worries." His polite smile is tragic beneath the fluorescent lights.

In a book he'd step into the elevator and be gone. In real life, he pushes the button then stands there, staring at the closed metal doors for long enough that I retreat into my office to escape the awkwardness. Eventually I hear the doors ping open and then closed.

My latte is cold and too sweet at the bottom, but I finish it anyway. Take my medicine in penance. The cookie bag stares up at me, as yet untouched. Looks like Olivia is getting a cookie. It would be gravel in my mouth.

Tattoo 2: Music Notes

"Heather?"

I look up from the apples I'm selecting to see Gina Martin, first chair clarinet at Oakmont Preparatory School. Always the seat to my left.

"Gina?" I say, as she leans in for a hug. "It's been years. How are you?"

"Well . . ." Gina says, sweeping a hand towards her belly, "I'm past the morning sickness, so that's something."

"You're pregnant?" I ask, staring from Gina's barely bumped stomach to her beaming face.

"Twenty weeks," she says. "Our first." I glance at the rings she flashes my way. Is it petty that I'm glad seem fingers are swollen? (You don't have to answer that.)

"Congratulations," I say. And I mean it. The band kids took me in when I transferred from public school to my step dad's alma mater freshman year. I didn't live for music like some of them, but having people, any people, to fit in with was huge. Yeah, we were "band geeks," but it didn't matter because we were geeks together.

"So what are you up to?" Gina asks. Her eyes have swept my tattoos, skipping quickly past the music notes on my collar bone.

"Oh, you know," I say. Not that she would have any reason to know. "I got my Ph.D. and I'm teaching linguistics at Springvale."

"Didn't you go to California for school?" she asks.

"I did," I say. "I came back."

Her eyes dart to my collarbone again.

Of all my tattoos, the music notes are the most "normal." The least offensive. But for Gina and the rest of our little group of friends, they're a reminder.

The silence has stretched too long.

"Congratulations again," I say. "I'm sure you'll have a lovely baby."

This is a clear dismissal, but Gina doesn't take it. Instead she reaches for my hand.

"I'm sorry, Heather," she says. Her eyes are glistening. "I'm sorry for not getting the tattoo. My parents said I couldn't, that it wasn't something our kind did."

"Our kind?" I ask, pulling my hand from hers.

She shrugs helplessly. "I'm sorry," she says again.

I am not going to cry in a grocery store. Instead I nod. Force a smile.

"I forgive you," I say. "It's no biggie."

It was though. It was a biggie when all of my friends backed out of our matching tattoos after I was permanently inked.

It's obvious Gina knows I'm lying, but she nods anyway and wipes at her eyes.

"Thank you, Heather," she says, leaning in and hugging me again. I awkwardly pat her shoulder.

"You were always the brave one," she says as she pulls back. Then she motions to her cart. "Better get this done if I want a nap this afternoon. Making a human really takes it out of you."

I smile and wave, just a little, as Gina pushes her cart away from produce.

The music notes are the only tattoo I regret.

Chapter 23
Coming Unzipped

I don't see Darcy on Tuesday or Wednesday afternoon, which means that when Wednesday night rolls around we haven't discussed our game plan going into dinner with the mothers.

I considered texting or emailing. It should be me, probably, with how we left things. But I don't. I'm going to assume the game plan is telling them the truth.

There's a knock on the front door at 5:55.

"Come in," I yell from my bedroom.

One advantage of living in a house the size of a postage stamp is that my voice easily covers the distance. You'd have to be a contortionist to get the dark teal sheath dress I'm wearing zipped all the way up, and Olivia is stuck at the lab again. Which means I've been hiding in my bedroom, away from our giant picture window, awaiting my mom's arrival.

"Mom, come back," I call stepping into the hallway.

And, of course, there he is. Darcy's in my entryway wearing a crisp tailored suit, just like you'd expect from a Delancey. His hands are in the pants pockets and his face goes from neutral to, huh, appreciative?, as he directs his perusal from my eat in kitchen to where I stand, half naked, at the end of a too well lit hallway.

Fine, I'm not half naked. I'm 88% dressed. But I'm barefoot and not zipped the last quarter of the way, which makes me feel exposed.

"You are not my mother," I say.

He gives me a look, head tilted to the side and a self-deprecating smile. "No. That I am not."

I still feel awkward from that unintentionally sent email, but if Darcy wants to pretend it never happened, I can do that.

"So how did you end up my ride?" I ask. Is Darcy blushing? Wait, shoot.

"The mothers thought it made more sense for me to pick you up since we live so close. And now that the secret's out about our relationship."

"I was expecting something more elaborate," I say.

"Well, that comes later," Darcy continues. "My mom has decided that she'll stay at your mother's house tonight, since it's closer to the airport."

"And the restaurant?"

"Northland."

"Of course. So you're driving me home as well."

"I am. Speaking of, we'd better go. Are you ready?"

He looks at my bare feet and I realize he can't tell I'm unzipped from there. Maybe I can slip into my room and somehow get this zipper . . . Who am I kidding? I need his help.

Be cool, Heather.

"I'm almost ready," I say. "But I need a zip."

His eyebrows shoot skyward.

"We aren't in the fifth grade, Delancey," I say. "You'll survive."

I grab my heals from the bedroom and stride down the hall. Somehow our eyes catch, and I don't know how to look away. When I reach Darcy, I'm stuck in his gaze until he clears his throat and I remember my dress is undone.

I turn my back to him and pull my hair to one side. He's seeing Mima's butterfly. All of it. I wonder what he think and then his knuckle skims along my skin, along the butterfly's delicate wing.

"It's beautiful," Darcy whispers.

"Thanks." My voice is low, matching his.

"Well, then," he says, "I'll just . . ." I feel the zipper rise and Darcy fumbles for a moment with the little hook at the top. "All done."

I take a deep breath then turn.

"You look lovely tonight, Heather," Darcy says. "It should be a crime to cover a work of art like that." He's too close and this is too . . . I don't know what. Too not me and Darcy.

I smirk up at him. "If you liked that one, you should see my ass," I say.

He snorts and gives me that familiar "I can't believe you just said that" smile. But then it turns. His eyes darken, and I wonder, for the first time ever, what it would be like to . . .

No. Heck to the no.

"Hold these," I say, pushing my glorious mustard heels into his chest. Then I retreat to the kitchen and grab my water bottle, purely to put some distance between us. "Want a water?" I call over my shoulder to where Darcy still stands in the hall.

"I'm sure they have that at the restaurant," he says with a glance at the clunky, sticker-covered metal bottle in my hands. It would look more appropriate in the backpack of a middle-schooler than it does with my outfit tonight, but that's not the issue. I rejoin Darcy, grabbing my wallet from my purse as I pass.

"Let's get this over with," I say as I lead the way out the door.

Chapter 24

Tesla

Darcy drives a Tesla. I know, you were thinking Prius. You forgot to factor in the "old money."

Unlike me, Darcy never fell from grace, whereas I stumbled down that hill for years before taking the plunge off the cliff. So while I got a lovely dinner with my mother and $1000 upon the completion of my PH.D., Darcy got a Model S.

I don't know much about cars, but I googled Darcy's the first time I saw him driving it. If we were keeping track, the Delanceys are about $79,000 ahead of my parents in the gifts department now.

And in case you were wondering, Darcy got his Tesla when owning one meant you cared about the environment and had no other political implications.

Regardless, riding in it is lovely. And it's ridiculously clean. I'm not flattered. I know what his desk looks like, so it's doubtful that's a sign of extra effort expended on my behalf. Still, it's nice.

"So what are we telling our mothers?" I ask. "I'm assuming the truth?"

Darcy's eyes are on the road ahead.

"About that," he says.

"Aren't you the one who said 'Whatever bears affinity to cunning is despicable'?"

"No. What I quoted was from later in the the story. The first proposal."

"Of course it was," I mutter. "The point is the same, Fitzwilliam."

Darcy sighs. "I'm sure you're right," he says.

"Wait. Can you repeat that?"

"What?"

"I'm sure there was a 'but' coming, but if I could just have a moment to bask in the first half of that sentence . . ." I smile sweetly at the side of Darcy's face, but he doesn't take his eyes from the road.

"I will acknowledge that your course of action is the most sensible," Darcy says. "However," (I love how he emphasizes not using the word "but") "My mother has become a horror. Now that our thirtieth birthdays are approaching, she's gone into overdrive. She was talking about signing me up on a dating app that screens by credit score, Heather. She offered to run my profile for me."

I can't help the laugh that escapes, and this time he does glance my way.

"I'm glad this amuses you," he says.

"Oh, it does," I say. "Is your credit perfect, Darcy? C'mon, tell me your number."

"I am not telling you my credit score," he says.

"Why not? It's going to be available for everyone to see."

"I don't think it works that way," he says. "Plus, that's what I'm trying to avoid."

"Handsome, eligible bachelor from a good family requires same. Must enjoy Jane Austen, Earl Grey tea and walks in the rain."

"I don't drink Earl Grey," Darcy says.

My attempts to stifle the laughter are ineffective.

"Fine," he says. "I knew this would amuse you. Forget I said anything."

"Hold on," I say, putting one hand up. "I'm pulling it together. Really."

I attempt a sip from my water bottle and barely get it down without snorting it out through my nose.

Darcy is shaking his head. "You know it's bad when dating you is the lesser of the evils," he says. I don't think he intends it to be insulting, but it stings, just a little.

"Fake-dating me," I say.

He shrugs, looking from me to the road, and a smile has formed on his face that I've never seen before. It combines incredulity and . . . fondness? Surely not.

"How long?" I ask.

"Maybe a month or two? Then we can tell them it just didn't work out."

"Wait. Them? Do you want me to lie to my mom too?"

"I don't think she'll keep the truth from my mother, do you?"

"No," I say. "Which means I can't do it. My mother is the only one in my family still talking to me, and I'm not risking that."

The words are out before I realize what I've said. This is not the kind of thing I tell Darcy. But I suppose it was the kind of thing I told F.W.

In the seat beside me, Darcy's gone silent.

"What if it was just for tonight?" he asks.

"What do you mean?"

"We stage the breakup tonight. I can be heartbroken for a while, and that will keep me safe until that app goes bankrupt. Or at least until I can figure out something else."

"Are you fake dumping me before we even start fake dating?" I ask.

He shrugs. "You can fake dump me instead," he says.

"You bet I will," I say. "And you're still going to have to drive me home."

"We work together, Heather. I'm sure we can manage to be civil."

"As civil as ever," I say.

He glances at me and I bear my teeth. This is going to be fun.

Chapter 25

The Break-Up

Darcy and I arrived at the restaurant before our mothers and were quickly seated at a table for four.

"So should we snipe at each other the whole time or go out with a bang after dessert?" I ask.

"Whichever you prefer, my darling. You know I aim only to make you happy."

"Passive aggressive it is," I say. Darcy gives me one of his teeth-showing smiles. In another world . . . but not this one.

"Well, kids, imagine meeting you here," Camilla says as they take their seats. I look questioningly to my mom who mimes taking a drink.

"You know, Heather," my mother says, "you might have mentioned that you and Darcy were getting to know each other before the ceremony on Saturday. Camilla and I wouldn't have had to strategize nearly so diligently."

"We've been 'getting to know each other' for years, Mom," I say. "But I wasn't sure how Darcy felt about making this new phase of our relationship public." I glance his way. "Sometimes I think I'm his dirty little secret."

At this Darcy sputters his drink through his nose and onto his bread plate. He looks from the puddle to me, horrified.

"Sorry about that, darling," I say with a grin that shows exactly how not sorry I am.

"At least it wasn't me this time," Camilla chimes in as she downs her champagne. "The Delancey's aren't generally known as spillers . . ."

While she contemplates this my mother flags down a passing waiter who has the offending plate removed and replaced in no time.

"Now, where were we?" I ask.

"I believe," Darcy says, "that you were impeaching my character. I would never want to keep you a secret. I just wanted to keep you all to myself."

My mother's hand flies reflexively to her heart. Geesh.

I take a sip of wine. "This is almost as dry as you, Darcy," I say. "You should try it."

I hand him my glass, red lipstick marking where my mouth had been. He looks at it then places his lips directly over the spot. A tingle runs from my toes to my stomach. What in the world?

"Delicious, darling," he says.

Across the table, our mothers beam.

My salmon is perfect, and Darcy insists I try his steak, which tastes like a steak. He's taking this couple thing a bit far, and when he asks if I'd like to split a dessert, it's all I can do not to stomp on his foot under the table. I order my own slice of chocolate cake then excuse myself to go to the restroom.

"I'll accompany you," Darcy says, rising.

Our mothers exchange yet another knowing look. What, do they think we're going to start making them grandchildren on the way to the restroom?

"This has gone well," Darcy says once we've put some distance between us and the table.

"It has," I say. Something in his tone is causing goose bumps on my skin. We go down a wood-paneled hallway and stop outside the ladies room door.

"This is me," I say.

Darcy glances at the door then keeps talking.

"There's nothing that says we have to break up at this dinner," he says.

He's standing close, looking down at me. This is what it would have been like if this were a real date . . . him on the porch of my bungalow . . .

I take a step back as his words register.

"What are you saying?" I ask.

Darcy shrugs. "I've had a nice time tonight, Heather."

"You've had a nice time tonight?"

"I have." His expression is open. Earnest, even.

"To clarify," because I have to get this right, "are you saying you actually want to date me, or that you want to continue this facade for our mothers?"

"I actually want to date you, Heather," he says.

"But . . . why?"

"Why?"

"Yeah, why? And why now?"

"Can't it just be that I enjoy your company?"

I laugh, incredulous.

"No, it cannot. Because last I checked, you weren't a masochist."

Darcy's eyes widen. "No, no I'm not," he says.

I stare at him for a second and then roll my eyes. "Oh my gosh, Fitzwilliam" I say. "I didn't mean it sexually."

His chuckles is awkward. "Lucky break, that."

I shake my head. "This has gotten off track. We're supposed to be out here breaking up. So why is it that now, after all this time, you want to date me?"

"You've seen how happy it makes our mothers," he says.

"You want to date me to make our mothers happy?" I ask. I'm all for a guy loving his mom, but this seems a bit extreme. And that's when the coin drops.

"It's because you know who I am," I say.

"Of course I know who you are," Darcy replies, oblivious to the fuse that's been lit.

"No," I say, "I mean that you now know I have the pedigree to fit into your classist society."

"What are you talking about?"

"I can't believe this," I say.

"Heather, this has nothing to do with 'pedigree.' We aren't dogs. If anything, 'now' is because I liked who I was emailing. It let me see a side of you I hadn't before."

This makes me pause. I loved getting to know F.W., even before I knew he was a he. I'm leaning against the wall, wondering if this could work, when an older woman in pearls and a satin pantsuit passes on her way into the restroom. Her gaze lingers on my lotus tattoo, lips

115

pursing. Reminding me of all the times I was too much or not enough for people whose opinions mattered to my parents.

I close my eyes to recenter myself

"I can't do it," I say.

"Can't do what?"

"I can't date you."

"But why?"

The look on his face isn't hurt. It's curious. Maybe even hopeful. Like he thinks he can change my mind. And maybe I'd have let him try if that woman hadn't passed and reminded me of all the ways I'd been cut before. Of how I tried so hard to make myself what they wanted that I didn't even know who I was anymore. And they still didn't accept me.

But I won't tell him that. Instead I offer the most shallow of truths.

"Because," I say, "I won't be sucked back into a world that says my father's blood isn't as good as my mother's. You're welcome to live your life in the classist Victorian era, but I'm going to live mine now."

"It's Georgian, and Regency," Darcy mumbles under his breath. I smirk, taking refuge in the familiarity of baiting him. This, at least, I understand. But something has shifted in Darcy. Is he . . . angry?

"You know what?" Darcy says, pinching the bridge of his nose like I've given him a headache. Maybe I have. "I'll own that. I love an era governed by courtesy and chivalry. There's nothing wrong with respect and politeness."

I scoff. "You mean fakeness and hypocrisy?"

"At least I live in this world," Darcy says. "Meanwhile you're living in the woods with elves and dragons in a time that never existed."

"Fantasy burn, Darcy?" I ask. But yeah, it did kind of hurt. I cross my arms. "I guess this makes us officially broken up," I say.

"Yeah," Darcy agrees. "It does." He takes a deep breath. "Let's go tell our mothers."

"I've still got to pee," I say, motioning my head towards the door.

The woman I saw outside smiles at me in the mirror as she washes her hands. Did I misread her? I force a smile back.

Once I'm in the stall, I sort back through what just happened. Did Darcy really want to date me? And I turned him down? Well, of course I did. Why would I ever want to date Darcy Delancey? The picture that pops into my head, with those beautiful blues lit up with laughter, well, that just isn't helpful.

When I exit the restroom, Darcy is waiting on me.

"You ok?" he asks.

"Why wouldn't I be?" I say.

He leans away from the wall and follows me back into the dining area. My mother eyes us warily as she picks up the check, but I shake my head. Camilla is oblivious to the change. Darcy will have to deal with that later.

The silence continues the entire ride home.

"Thanks for that," Darcy says as I exit the car.

I lift my doggie bag with its barely-touched piece of chocolate cake. "It wasn't for nothing," I say.

Our forced grins match.

I close the door and retreat to my house, wondering how doing exactly what we meant to do had turned out so badly.

Tattoo 13: Fairy in the Rain

You know that $250 mom gave me instead of a Tesla? Well, it became a lovely fairy using an umbrella to keep the sprinkling crystal rain from her wings.

It's on my lower back, right where Darcy's seat warmer hit.

Would he have liked it? He liked Mima's butterfly . . . called it beautiful.

I guess we'll never know.

Chapter 26
Scandal

"Did you hear?" Olivia asks.

She's in my bedroom doorway while I sit at my desk writing. Normally, I'd point towards the sign hanging on the wall above me that threatens dragon fire to those who interrupt the author. But who are we kidding? Writing is getting me nowhere today.

"What is it I haven't heard?" I ask Olivia, pushing my chair back from the desk.

"Dean Mitchell is retiring," she says.

"Really?" This has implications. Dean Mitchell, who I see once every two weeks at department meetings and absolutely never outside of them, is technically my direct report.

"Really," Olivia says. "But that's not the big news . . ."

"That's pretty big news," I say.

"Yeah, but the bigger news, or maybe biggest news?" She's searching her marvelous physics-oriented brain for an answer that will make perfectly logical sense and be utterly opposed to the common laws and usage of grammar.

"Olivia?" I pull her back. She blinks at me a couple times and then goes on.

"Scandal," she says, making her eyes comically wide.

"Scandal?" I ask. "Has my entire life turned into an Austen novel?" I'm trying to write fantasy here.

"Scandal that would make Jane Austen blush," Olivia says.

"That really wouldn't take much," I say. "They were pretty easily scandalized back then. Kind of by stuff we think of as normal. Was he sleeping with a student or something?"

"Ew. No."

"Are you going to tell me, or am I going to go back to writing?"

Olivia glances at my computer where the open document has exactly seven words.

"I think I'll let you get back to writing," she says with a nonchalant shrug. "Wouldn't want the dragons to get me."

"My flow is broken," I say, closing the incriminating screen. "Tell me."

As Olivia tells me, my jaw falls. I can't repeat it. This will be the biggest cover-up in the history of Springvale University, and I won't leak it, in a novel, no less, even under the guise of fiction. But take whatever scandal you think is worst then multiply it by ten and subtract the common denominator of pi and no frigging way and you'll be about there.

It's nearly impossible to believe this of the boring man who's led our meetings for the past five years, but Olivia's source is too good to refute.

"Do you think Darcy knows?" I finally ask.

Olivia gives me a look.

"What?" I ask. "He's been mentored by the man from day one."

"I don't know," Olivia says. "You'll just have to ask him."

"I can't ask him," I say. "You said I can't tell a soul."

"True," Olivia says. "Maybe you can do some fishing though, and find out."

"I was planning to avoid him as much as possible," I say. "You know, since the fake break-up."

"It was fake," Olivia says.

"Yeah, but some of the things we said were a little too real."

I think of his jab about me burying myself in imaginary worlds. Once again, Darcy was a bit too clear of a mirror.

"Well, if he gets the job you'll barely have to see him at all," Olivia says.

"What do you mean?"

"Well, I doubt they'd make the Dean office in a basement," she says.

"You mean if Darcy gets the job? What about if I get the job?" I ask.

"Do you want the job?" Olivia looks genuinely confused. "Because I'm team Heather all the way if you do, but it sounds like more work to me. A bunch of butt kissing and paperwork and meetings with bigwigs."

"That doesn't seem like my style, does it?" I ask.

"Olivia shakes her head. "Thankfully, no. Can you imagine yourself at donor dinners every other weekend?"

"I'd rather be trapped in Orthanc," I say.

Olivia looks at me blankly.

"Come on," I say. "You watched the Lord of the Rings with me. The tower where Saruman trapped Gandolf?"

"Let's go out for dinner," Olivia says. "You've obviously been spending too much time in the Shire."

"I went out on Wednesday," I say.

"Fine," she says. "I've been spending too much time in the lab."

I'm ashamed to say this, but this is the first time in the conversation that I've actually really looked at Olivia. Like, looked at her to see her. She's less buoyant than normal, and there are shadows under her eyes.

"Are you sure you're up for going out?" I ask. "You look like you should be falling asleep to a chic flick."

"No, I'm good. Can we go to Fi's Place?" she asks.

Fiona's is a favorite with professors on a Friday night, and I wonder if Olivia has an ulterior motive. But I don't press. Just agree.

"Give me five minutes," I say with a glance down at my pajamas.

"Take ten," Olivia says. Her smile doesn't look rejuvenated, but resigned. "I'll just take a nap while I wait."

I glance back at my closed computer. My heroine will have to wait. My real life best friend obviously needs me, even if she won't tell me why.

Chapter 27

Fiona's

It's not until we walk into Fiona's that I realize how long it's been since I've been out on a Friday night.

So, yeah, I was out last Saturday. But this is different from a room where the average age is in the high sixties and the commonality is a love for Jane Austen.

Fi's Place is packed from entryway to cornhole yard with twenty and thirty somethings. It's warm for September, and much of the exposed skin sports tattoos, but not in a biker bar way. In a drunk at a frat party ten years ago way. The energy is loud and slightly frantic, reminding me why I don't go out on Friday nights.

Not long ago I could relax into this. Let the energy buoy me up. But now . . . A glance at Olivia reminds me that I'm not here for myself.

Olivia is staring intently around the space.

"C'mon," she says, grabbing my arm and pulling me forward. I follow her through the crowded restaurant and out a back door onto the patio where she plants us, oh so casually, beside a table where the women are gathering their purses and starting to stand. We only lurk for about thirty seconds before they leave and we're able to snag the table, un-bussed dishes and all.

"I still don't know how you do that," I say.

Olivia shrugs. "It's a gift."

It truly is.

"You keep the table, I'll go get food?" I ask.

"Sure," she says. "Burnt ends."

"Want to split sweet potato fries?" I ask.

"What kind of question is that?" It's good to see she's gotten some of her spark back.

I make my way through the crowd to the queue by the kiosks.

"You never called," says a voice at my shoulder. Looking up I see Benji, the tatted up barista from the Cranky Bean.

"What was your name again?" I ask.

"Benji."

"That's right," I say. I really am very good at names, whether I want to be or not. But Benji doesn't need to know that. "Well, Benji, I have a policy of not dating students. It's frowned upon as unprofessional."

"I'm a fifth year," Benji says. "Way past legal."

"Is this your last semester?" I ask.

He looks like he might lie, then he relents. "I'll graduate in May," he says.

"Well then, Benji, if you happen to run into me after that, you can ask again." I smile. He does seem like a nice enough kid, despite not eating sugar, so I'm trying to brush him off kindly.

"Can I at least buy you a drink?" he asks.

I shake my head no. "Not going to happen, Benji." He stands there awkwardly for a moment then excuses himself from the food queue and makes for the bar.

I eventually get a kiosk and order, then I wait another few minutes to pick up our Moscow mules from the bar before carrying them and the metal holder with our order number back to the patio. I'd feel guilty for leaving Olivia alone this long, but it couldn't be helped. I expect to find her on her phone, but when I return she's chatting with Andrew Chu, of all people and . . . heck no. That is not –

Darcy Delancey looks good casual. Like, really good. Even better than when he's dressed up. Dang it. I'm not prepared for what my stomach is doing at the sight of him in jeans.

He's risen now and is taking a drink and the number sign from my hand. He places it beside another order number sign that's already on the table and hands the mule to Olivia.

"Look who I found," Olivia says.

"Technically, I think we found you." This is from Andrew.

"Is it alright if we join you?" Darcy asks, still standing. He looks worried, like I might say no. And really, I'd consider it. But a quick glance around shows me that, if anything, Fi's Place is even more packed than it was when we arrived.

"Of course," I say. Olivia looks relieved, but I can't understand why. Isn't she supposed to hate Andrew as much as I hate Darcy? Even as I think it I realize I don't really hate Darcy anymore. Inconvenient, that.

"So what brought you out tonight?" I ask Darcy and Andrew.

"The end of the season cornhole tournament, of course," Andrew says, nodding at something over my shoulder. Sure enough, a giant chalkboard is hanging from the outside privacy fence. On it is a bracket with sixteen team names.

"We're 'Schooled-you, Tosser," Andrew says. "Since we're professors."

"It only works if you don't have to explain it," Olivia says. And why is it I wish she'd just let it pass?

"So this is a thing, huh? Did you have to earn your way in, or just sign up?" I ask.

"I'm afraid if I tell you, you'll mock me," Darcy says.

"I would never, Fitzwilliam," I reply. "Or, at least, I wouldn't mock Andrew."

Andrew laughs. "We were in a league," he says. "Darcy and I have spent way too many Friday nights here playing cornhole."

"And I thought you were home washing your hair," I say.

Darcy looks at me like he has no idea what that means. Really, I don't either.

"So, you've worked for this all season and tonight's the big night. I'm glad we randomly ended up here to cheer you on." I say this with a pointed look at Olivia who's staring down into her mule.

"I let everyone know at this week's staff meeting," Andrew says. "Darcy was supposed to too."

"I must have forgotten," Darcy says.

I chuckle at the idea of Darcy ever making such an announcement. Then I remember the dean.

"Wait," I say. "Did you hear about Dean Mitchell?"

"What about him?" Darcy asks.

I dart a look at Olivia, who's does a quick and violent shake of her head.

"Nothing," I say. "Nothing that can't wait until after your tournament, anyway." Darcy's studying me, and I know he'll get it out of me if I don't do something drastic, and soon.

"We could help you warm up," I say.

I know this will cost us our cushy table. We'll be eating barbeque standing up and leaning against a wall. But it's worth it when I see the relief on Olivia's face.

"Sure," Andrew says. "They've got a couple of lines reserved for tournament entrants. I'll go put our names on the list."

As Andrew rises, a waitress arrives with the guys' orders. I insist Darcy not wait, despite his desire to be a gentleman. I steal a fry from his plate. "I'm going to keep eating these," I say. "You'd better get started."

He takes the biggest fry from the pile and dips it in bbq sauce before folding it into his mouth. Not that I'm watching. I raise my eyes from his mouth and realize I'm caught.

Darcy's look is all question. Before I can answer, the waitress returns with Olivia and my orders.

"Sweet potato fries are better," I say, popping one into my mouth.

Darcy just smiles.

Chapter 28

Cornhole champions

We end up with the best of both worlds. There's plenty of time to finish our dinners sitting down before it's the guys' turn to warm up on the cornhole court. Andrew even has time to get another round of drinks for the table. Darcy's is water. Apparently he takes his cornhole seriously. My second mule tastes as good as the first, if not better.

Olivia has a second as well, which is odd for her. Our running joke is that there's no such thing as two-drink Olivia, because she's gone to sleep. But apparently not tonight.

I blame alcohol for what happens next. Not the fact that we decide to play guys vs. girls to warm them up for the tournament. Not that I end up on one side with Darcy while Olivia is on the other with Andrew. No. Those things would have happened anyway.

But Olivia shoving Andrew with more strength than I would have thought encased in her tiny body? That I blame on the second Mule and years of pent-up animosity.

Seeing his six foot form sprawling across a neighboring cornhole board, I can't help but flash back to my brother's rehearsal dinner. But Olivia doesn't bend down to console him. No. She throws the rest of her Moscow Mule, which really, still looks nearly full, at his startled face and storms into the restaurant.

Darcy and I exchange a glance and, surprisingly, my first instinct isn't to throw my drink in his face in solidarity.

"I'm going after Olivia," I say. Darcy nods, already striding Andrew's direction.

A quick scan of the restaurant's interior gives no sign of her. I walk into the restroom rather than out the front doors, since we took my car.

"Olivia," I call, forcing a smile for a woman fixing her makeup in one of the mirrors.

"In here," Olivia says. She walks out of a stall dabbing folded toilet paper at her eyes.

"Sad or pissed?" I ask. Olivia is an angry crier.

"That Andrew Chu needs to learn when to keep his mouth shut," she says in reply.

"Pissed, then," I say. "What happened?"

Olivia's eyes dart to the woman who's still staring into the mirror, listening flagrantly, with no attempt at hiding it.

"Sorry," she says, putting the mascara in her purse. Olivia and I don't speak again until the door closes behind her.

"So what happened?" I ask. "Surely he wasn't just giving you crap about our cornhole score." It had been rather pathetic.

"No, he was giving you crap about our cornhole score," she says. "Which, whatever. But then he said that was why Darcy could never date you."

"What?"

"Yeah, that's what I said," Olivia says. "And then Andrew says 'oh, I was just joking. But Darcy would never date her with all those tattoos. His parents would freak.'"

"And then you pushed him over?" I ask.

"No. Then I told him that any man who would let his parents dictate who he could and couldn't date needed to grow a pair."

I sputter a laugh, imagining those words from sweet Olivia's mouth.

"And then you pushed him over?" I ask again.

"And then I pushed him over." She lets out a long breath. "It may have been an over-reaction."

"You think?" I study my friend's face. Something is off.

"You're aware that my mother and Camilla Delancey have been plotting my wedding to Darcy since before we were born, right?"

"I am," Olivia says. "But apparently stupid Andrew Chu didn't get the memo."

"Why are you really so mad?" I ask.

Her lip begins to quiver, and then Olivia is crying. Not angry this time. And not just a little bit.

"Oh, honey, come here," I say, pulling her into a hug.

Two women walk into the bathroom, one heading to the stalls, the other to the sink. Olivia burrows her face further into my shoulder as they pass.

"It's just not fair, you know?" she asks after a couple awkward moments of me stroking her back and telling her it's going to be ok. I hope that's true. Eventually she's pulled herself together enough to straighten her tiny shoulders.

"I will never be Asian," she says. My glance darts to the tall black woman washing her hands at the sink. She looks from Olivia's tiny blonde self to me and raises an eyebrow. I give a small shrug and refocus on Olivia.

"That's true," I say. "Have you ever wanted to be Asian?"

"I mean, maybe, in my Mulan phase, but that's not the point," Olivia says. I wait. She sighs. "Andrew only dates Asians. Because his parents are first generation, and it matters to them."

"When did you learn that?" I ask. More importantly, why is Olivia crying over this? Since when has she wanted to date Andrew?

"One of the groom's sisters told me," Olivia says. "At the wedding. Apparently her best friend crushed on Andrew Chu all through high school, but when she invited him to the ladies choice dance, he told her he could only date Asians or he'd break his mother's heart. And we were getting along really well, too." Olivia's face has fallen, and I struggle for words as I let the universe realign itself around me. Olivia and Andrew?

"Girl, she was lying."

Olivia and I both turn to the woman at the sink.

"Excuse me?" I ask.

"You're talking about the Andrew Chu who's a physics professor at Springvale, right?"

"Yes."

"Tina, you still in there?" the woman calls.

"Coming out now." A lovely, dark-skinned woman in jeans and a halter top exits the stall and heads to the sink.

"You dated Andrew Chu, right?" our good Samaritan asks.

"A couple of times," Tina says. "Nice guy, but we didn't click."

The first woman raises that expressive eyebrow again.

"You don't happen to be Asian?" Olivia asks.

Tina laughs as she grabs paper towels from the dispenser. "Not last I checked," she says.

"So either Andrew lied in high school or the groom's sister lied when she saw you two hitting it off," says the first woman. "Either way, you don't have to be Asian to date Andrew Chu."

Olivia, my normally introverted best friend, throws her arms around the random stranger. Staring up she says "Thank you!" with a beaming smile, which the woman returns less enthusiastically.

"Go get 'em, honey," the woman says, patting Olivia on the shoulder as she and Tina leave the bathroom. Olivia stares at their retreating backs.

"When did you start liking Andrew?" I ask. "This is not acceptable."

"When did you start liking Darcy?" she replies.

"I don't."

Olivia gives me a look. Apparently her newfound hope is making her see things that aren't there.

"You have a funny way of showing it," she says. "You obviously didn't mind finding him at our table."

"The place is packed. I couldn't very well make him leave," I say. Suddenly Olivia's face falls.

"Oh no!" she says. "I pushed Andrew over."

"And threw a drink in his face," I say. Because I'm helpful like that. "You also told him to grow a pair."

Olivia groans. "I'm just going to stay here," she says. "Forever."

I take her by the shoulders and look deep into her eyes.

132

"You will never be Asian," I say. "But you will also not be a bathroom dweller on my watch."

I turn her towards the exit.

"Let's go."

Chapter 29

Crap and Double Crap

I follow Olivia back through the crowded restaurant to the equally crowded patio. Laughter and clinking glass and the occasional shout are layered over the music of a 90's alternative band that I haven't heard of in decades.

We find Andrew and Darcy seated on a bench along the fence. Andrew has one leg up with a bag of ice on his ankle. He eyes Olivia warily.

"Will you still be able to play?" she asks.

Andrew places his foot on the ground, puts a little weight on it. He may wince, but not much.

"I think I'll be fine," he says.

"I'm really sorry," Olivia says. "Do you think we could talk for a minute?"

Andrew shoots a glance at Darcy.

"Competition doesn't start for another fifteen," Darcy says. "And we're not playing in the first set."

Andrew nods and looks back at Olivia. "I can talk. Do I need to be afraid?"

"I don't think so," Olivia says. Holy smokes, is she biting her lip? Andrew's gaze seems caught as well.

"Use my car," I say, handing Olivia the keys. While the patio is still warm enough from all of the heat lamps and bodies, anywhere they could speak privately is going to be outside and cold.

"Thanks," Olivia says. She leads Andrew back through the crowd."

"Like a lamb to the slaughter," says Darcy, propping one arm along the back of the bench.

"What does that mean?" I ask as I take the seat beside him. I turn at a right angle, one leg folded up, so I'm facing him and his arm isn't behind me.

"It means," says Darcy, "that Andrew is either about to become the happiest of men, in which case he will be willingly sacrificing his singlehood and all the benefits entailed, or he's about to be driven to a secondary location. And we all know the odds of coming back from that."

I laugh. "My money's on the first one," I say. "Despite the show a few minutes ago."

Darcy and I sit in awkward silence. I assume he wants to ask what the pushing and drink throwing was all about, but he doesn't. I appreciate that. Obviously, I can't tell him. If Olivia and Andrew work things out, Andrew can tell him what he wants to. The idea of Olivia and Andrew being a couple bringing Darcy and me together flits into my head. I kick it out.

"I didn't know you and Andrew were friends," I say. It's not a question exactly, but I'm hoping he'll volunteer some information.

"It's a cornhole thing," Darcy says with a shrug. I give him a look. "What, he's really good," Darcy says.

"And I suppose you're really good too?" I ask, bumping him with my foot.

He shrugs again, a little smile on his lips. And holy crap, I see it. In fact, I'm hit in the face with it. This is what Olivia was talking about . . . I am flirting with Darcy Delancey. Someone kill me now.

"I need a drink," I say, standing. "Can I get you something?"

"Actually," Darcy pulls my Moscow Mule from below the bench, "I grabbed this when you followed Olivia, if you still want it."

The sweetness of the gesture does mushy things to my insides. Not cool, Heather.

"I'm sure it's diluted by now," I say. This may or may not be true, but I need an excuse to get away from here, even if it's just for a couple of minutes. Besides, Andrew bought that one. So I'm really only paying for two.

Darcy looks at the drink in his hand, as though considering arguing with me about its suitability, or maybe wondering what to do with it now.

"Here," I take it from his hand. "I'll drop it off in a bus tub on my way to the bar. Are you sure you don't need anything?"

I can't interpret the look he's giving me. And I'm doubly annoyed by the fact that I'm trying.

"No," he says. "I'm good. I'll just hold down the bench."

"Sounds good," I say, turning and fleeing like the nine riders are on my tail.

I think I hear Darcy chuckle, but I don't turn to check.

Chapter 30

The fires of love

Olivia and Andrew pass me while I'm waiting on my drink. They don't see me. I don't think they're seeing anything or anyone. Their hands are clasped together, and he's leaning down, way down, to hear something she's saying. Then he turns and suddenly he's piggy-backing her through the crowded room. I might vomit from the cuteness.

By the time I have my drink and am back on the patio, the guys are at a cornhole court and Olivia is alone on the bench.

"So." I say.

She grins. "Yeah."

I roll my eyes.

"You know we're still in Kansas City, right?"

"Yeah," she says again.

"And you're sure you don't hate him?"

"Not a bit."

I'm silent a moment, assessing my friend's joy.

"Good for you," I say.

"Good for us," Olivia says.

"For you and Andrew?" I ask.

"For you and me," she says.

"And why's that? I'll have more time to write while you're staying 'late at the lab,' or whatever you kids are calling it nowadays?"

"Nope," she says. Her gaze flits pointedly to Darcy. When I follow it, I find him smiling right at us. I cross my eyes at him and he grins before paying attention to the announcer who's getting this round started.

"That is not going to happen," I say.

Olivia shrugs. "I hear there's nothing like forced proximity to stoke the fires of love."

Chapter 31

Montage

We're going to montage this chapter, because I don't think I could handle revisiting it in prose after having to live through it.

Scene one: Coming into the house to find Andrew rubbing Olivia's feet while they watch reality television. Both look besotted.

Scene two: Kitchen; Olivia is picking noodles out of Andrew's hair. The remaining pasta is still in the pan. I'm hungry enough not to ask questions, but only finish half of my Pad Thai before the wondering is too much. I dump the rest in the trash.

Scene three: Stumbling down the dark hallway in the middle of the night to retrieve my water bottle from the living room. Andrew and Olivia are asleep on the couch. He's laying behind her, his arm around her waist, holding her close. My shields are down, in my half-awake state, and I can admit that I want this. I want it so badly. I snatch up my water bottle and return to my bed, but it's a long time before I fall asleep.

Tattoo 5: The Dragonfly

I had a crush on Andy Fairbanks from second to ninth grade. Then I dated him. By dated, I mean we called ourselves a couple and made out on the bus to band camp.

My friends didn't like his friends ("the drum line thinks they're better than everyone else"), and our love, as it was, couldn't withstand the factions dividing us.

Andy didn't get his own tattoo. He would have, I'm sure, if I'd been allowed to get a tattoo between second and ninth grade. But he was a valuable lesson about the difference between fantasy and reality. Between what you think you want and what you really want. I thought of him while lying on the table having a gorgeous dragonfly inked across the left half of my stomach.

The dragonfly symbolizes self-realization and maturity. Wasn't twenty year old me cute? I got it when, after several short and lousy dating experiences (I wouldn't call them relationships) I decided to put away the pursuit of romantic love in favor of a more attainable dream: agent representation and a manuscript sold to a major publishing house.

See. Cute.

One day, twenty year old me, I will revel in your naivete. But I'm not there yet.

The dragonfly hurt worse than any tattoo I'd gotten thus far. It could have been because of the placement, the sheer size, the intricacy of the design. But more likely it was because I was killing one dream in favor of another. And death, in all its forms, is painful.

Chapter 32

Anything you can do

. . .

Late Wednesday afternoon, after a delightful nap in my office, I step out of the elevator into the main lobby. Darcy is there, chatting with Dean Mitchell whose back is to me. Probably just as well, as I'm pretty sure I'm scowling.

The Dean claps Darcy on the shoulder, says something that causes both to laugh, and leaves through the front doors. Darcy watches him go, then turns towards me as I approach.

"Heather," he says with a smile. "How are you?"

"How can you act like that around him after what he did?" I ask.

Darcy looks genuinely confused. "Around Dean Mitchell?"

I scan the empty lobby then give Darcy a "duh" look that would have made middle school me proud.

Darcy's sigh is long-suffering.

"I don't know what you heard," Darcy says, "but he's not retiring because he did something wrong. He's retiring because his wife wants to be closer to their grandchildren."

"Sure she does," I say.

"Think what you want, Heather. Some of us choose to believe the best about people. Even when they prove us wrong time and time again."

I ignore this obvious allusion to yours truly.

"Fine. Cover for him," I say with a shrug. "That's what the good ol' boys club is for, right?"

We've started walking towards the exit. Darcy looks sideways at me as he speaks.

"Are you aware that 75% of this department is female?"

"I am." (No, I wasn't.) "But the dean is always a man." I say it with confidence, despite having no idea whether or not it's true.

"The dean before Mitchell was a woman," Darcy says. "And so was the dean before that."

Shoot. We've reached the door, and Darcy holds it open the old fashioned way rather than pressing the handicap activation button. I walk before him into a frigid wind. The temperature has dropped thirty degrees since I entered the building after lunch the way it sometimes does in Kansas City. I hunch in on myself, tying my jacket's belt tight and wishing I'd chosen something heavier.

"I think we need to get it to 75%," I say.

"Get what?"

"You said the department is 75% female. The next dean needs to be female to keep the ratio on point."

"Maybe the next dean needs to be a man to keep things fair," Darcy says. "Fifty/fifty."

"They've opened it up to internal hires first." I glance his way and find his eyes on me.

143

"You don't even like teaching," he says slowly.

I shrug. "Maybe I'll like deaning better."

We walk a few more steps in silence, headed towards the staff parking lot. Dang, it's cold. I shouldn't have worn these heels either.

"Are you saying this to spite me?" Darcy asks.

Of course I am. I one hundred percent do not ever want to be dean. Just the thought of schmoozing with rich alumnae makes me want to go home and shower.

But I won't tell him that. Instead I say "Fitzwilliam, your ego knows no bounds."

He looks at me and looks away, all smug and warm in his long wool coat. Darcy Delancey, always perfectly attired for any situation. He'd probably enjoy donor dinners.

"Why *do* you teach?" Darcy asks.

"Excuse me?"

"That came out badly, but the question was genuine. Why did you go into teaching?"

"I don't think anyone's actually asked me that," I say. Darcy just waits. Finally I shrug. "You know what they say about those who can't."

"You can't 'linguize'?" Darcy asks.

"I don't appreciate the skepticism, Professor Delancey," I say. "Not everyone can linguize."

Darcy pushes bravely on. "What does someone with a linguistics degree do if they don't teach? What are the career paths?"

Now it's my turn to sigh. I hope it seems long-suffering, but I haven't perfected those the way he has. Truthfully, I haven't had as much reason to. But we don't need to get into that.

"There are a lot of options," I say, "mostly involving research, which I hate. Unfortunately, I didn't know that until midway through my MBA. I was just intrigued by the creation of language. How it impacts cultures, subcultures, the very thoughts we think . . . The words we use frame everything."

Darcy stops walking, so I stop too. He's staring at me like I've grown wings. Or maybe like he's just seen the white of Gandalf's robe shimmering beneath the grey outer cloak. Like I'm something impressive that he hasn't noticed before.

And I don't know what to do with that.

"If you brought that to your classroom, your students would come alive," Darcy says softly.

"Yeah," I agree. I start walking. "And then they'd show up at my office hours, and I'd never get to nap in peace."

Darcy snorts. It's the least cultured sound I've ever heard him make.

And unfortunately, I like it.

Chapter 33

Forced proximity

And that's how I roped myself into the running for next Dean of Humanities.

Because I was not backing out once Darcy thought I wanted the job. That is not my style. No, apparently I'd rather write application essays like an undergrad and go to interviews and kiss the backsides of the senior administration than admit I was just messing with Darcy Delancey.

And do you want to know the cherry on top?

In order to prove both leadership potential and the ability to play well with others, all internal applicants must collaborate on a project. That's right. Darcy and I, as well as Annette from psychology and Timothy from classics are coming up with a presentation about a joint vision for the department to be shown at Dean Mitchell's retirement party.

Let's pause for a moment and discuss these new characters, shall we?

First, Professor Annette Pfisten. She was a full professor when Darcy and I arrived five years ago. Some would say she was "passed over" when Dean Mitchell was given the job. Others would say there was a good reason. That reason has nothing to do with intelligence. She's brilliant. Unfortunately, she has this way of looking at you from behind sexy librarian glasses (please note, she is not a sexy librarian. She just has the glasses) and making you think that she is accurately judging every blemish on your soul. Frankly, donors don't want to be around her. And a major part of the job of "Dean" is "figurehead."

Then there's Professor Timothy Arrington III. Timothy Arrington III, or Timothy to his friends, makes Darcy look like a frat boy. I can only believe Timothy has been dressed in tweed from the cradle. He comes from a long line of Classics professors, most of whom made Dean by thirty, which means that he's at least a couple years behind schedule. If anything, that has shoved the stick farther . . . well, you get the picture.

To say our first meeting went badly would be a gross understatement.

This is the point where I admit there's not only a lovely butterfly tattoo dedicated to my Mima on my shoulder, but also a chip. One might say a large chip. And this specific gathering of people was designed to knock it off. Add to that the fact that I did not get my afternoon nap (thanks to Darcy's groupies) nor my afternoon coffee (I've been avoiding Benji who looks at me with puppy dog eyes every time I'm in the Cranky Bean) and it was a perfect storm.

Picture this. I arrive exactly on time to find Darcy, Tweed and the Not-Sexy Librarian already in the conference room. Someone (my money's on Darcy) has brought cookies and bottled water. There's a paper cup with my name on it at the one remaining seat. My eyes dart to Darcy.

"Benjamin says hello," Darcy says with a smirk. I roll my eyes but can't help the grin that creases my mouth. When did Darcy and I develop an inside joke? I sit, thinking this meeting might not be as terrible as I'd assumed.

While I'm getting settled in, Annette pushes the cookie box my way. It bumps up against my coffee, knocking it over. All that hot liquid glory pours out onto the table, and in slow motion I watch it make its way across the flat plane until it spills over the edge. Directly into my lap. It's only when I feel the burning that time resumes and I jump backwards. By then my ironically houndstooth skirt is drenched.

The sense of loss I feel is beyond all proportion. And for me, loss equals anger.

I raise my eyes to Annette. She's perfectly calm, and the side of her mouth is twitching, as though she's forcing herself to contain a smile. Oh, it's on.

"I'm so sorry," Annette says, rising slowly from her seat. "Let me get some paper towels."

"That was intentional," I say. It doesn't matter that I got this skirt from the clearance rack at J.C. Penney for a costume party and this is the first time I've worn it since. You don't go pouring coffee on people.

"What a ridiculous accusation," Annette says. "I won't dignify it with a response." Her back is towards me, but I swear I hear barely suppressed glee in her voice.

I glance Darcy's way, hoping to find an ally (the irony is not lost on me), but he looks dumbfounded. On my other side Timothy Tweed smirks down at his phone. I can't tell if he finds this situation amusing, or if he's oblivious to what's going on in the room in favor of a cat video, or whatever the tik tok algorithm has programmed for his entertainment. Either way, it pisses me off further.

"Timothy, did you see what just happened?" I ask.

He glances up. "Clumsy today?"

I have no words. Annette shoves paper towels into my hands.

"Clean yourself up," she says. "We've already waited long enough for you to get here."

"I was on time," I reply as I sop at my drenched skirt. Darcy has risen and gotten more towels. He cleans the table in front of me and re-centers the cookies.

"I'm afraid you'll regret that, Annette," he says in a friendly voice. "Heather is much more pleasant after coffee."

I scowl. Yeah, he's just trying to return us all to a lighter footing, but is that why he brought me coffee? He has lost all favor points the act would have gained him. In fact, I'm taking back the points coffee earned him in the past. He's in the red now in my book.

"We should get started," Timothy says, putting his phone face down on the table. "Obviously this whole thing is a formality, but we still want to prove our competence. We will be working together moving forward, after all."

"A formality?" I ask. I'm distracted, holding a soggy mass of paper towels that has done nothing to dry my skirt. In fact, now that the coffee is luke-warm, it gives the uncomfortable impression that I've peed myself. Darcy, ever the gentleman, takes my handful of towels and throws them away before resuming his seat. Fine. He's back to neutral.

I direct another scowl at Annette, but it's wasted as she's no longer paying any attention to me. Instead she's leaned back in her seat, arms crossed and eyes narrowed, all of her focus on Tweed.

"Can you expound on that, Professor Arrington?" Annette asks, her voice glacial.

"They have to go through the process so everything looks official," Timothy says. "But they've already made their decision. I'm sure it was done before the job was posted."

"And who have they decided on?" Annette asks.

Timothy snorts. "Not you."

If possible, Annette's lips purse even tighter.

After such an illustrious beginning, is it possible to say the meeting went downhill from there? After two hours of "my major is better than/ more valuable to society than/ more profitable than" yours conversations, I was ready to withdraw from the running. I might have done so (I don't actually want the job), except that if I do, Tweed or the Librarian would be that much closer to being my boss. And even working for Darcy would be better than that.

Chapter 34

The Brilliant Strategist

"You should form an alliance," Olivia says around a mouthful of pita bread and hummus. When I got home from the meeting from Hades (shout out Tweed), Olivia and Andrew were just sitting down to a meal of Mediterranean takeout. After a quick shower and change into pajama bottoms and a hoodie, I've joined them.

"I think you've been watching too much reality tv," I tell Olivia, accepting the plate Andrew passes my way. I haven't decided yet if Andrew's a super-nice guy with a gifts love language or if he's a brilliant strategist, but the amount of free take-out I've eaten since they started dating means that I don't care. Andrew is welcome here.

"If you're really going through with this" Olivia says, "you and Darcy need to team up."

I roll my eyes. "And you, Andrew?" I ask. "What's your opinion on this."

He looks from Olivia to me and then shrugs. "I agree with Olivia, of course."

"See!" Olivia crows. "Two to one . . . Alliance." She's looking at me like *Duh, point proven*, and I can't really fight the logic. At least not with all of the fighting I've just endured at that blasted meeting. Instead I take way longer than needed to chew my chicken before finally swallowing.

"What would forming an alliance entail?" I ask on a sigh.

"Oh, it could be so many things," Olivia says. "But we really should have Darcy here for this."

"I can't see Darcy tonight," I say. "I'm all peopled out. In fact, don't be offended, but I'm going to take this chicken and go hide in my room for the rest of the night." With that I rise, swiping another peace of pita from the bag and laying it on top of my plate.

"When's your next meeting?" Andrew asks.

"I've got three more Mondays of this torment before we present at the Dean's farewell party November 2nd."

"So, meeting this Friday would be plenty of time?" It's only now that I realize Andrew's texting.

"Did you just schedule an alliance meeting with Darcy Delancey on my Friday night?" I ask.

"Yep," Andrew says. "You're welcome."

That is so not what I meant. "Don't either of you have a life?"

"She's sitting beside me," Andrew says. I make an exaggerated gagging noise, unwilling to admit that, yes, it's cute and I wouldn't accept someone who thought Olivia deserved any less. "Besides," Andrew continues, "Friday was cornhole night. Now that the tournament's over, Darcy and I are both free."

"Did you stop to think I might not be?"

Olivia, the traitor, laughs. I shoot her a glare, but it does nothing.

"Fine," I say. "But one of you is bringing dinner."

Andrew looks pointedly at the plate of food in my hand. "I'll tell Darcy it's his turn," he says.

"Good," I say. "Tell him no Indian food."

"Why?" Andrew asks. "Isn't that his favorite?"

"Exactly."

I'm considering an alliance for the greater good. That doesn't mean Darcy gets to enjoy it.

Chapter 35

The War Room

"Hold the door!" I call as I sprint down the murder hallway.

Sprint is an exaggeration. It's more of a zombie shuffle as my heel, not fully in my shoe, crushes stiff red pleather with every step. The bag on my shoulder shifts, nearly falling.

I napped too long, and the brain fog won't clear. This would be worth it if the beautifully crafted prose that were flowing so freely in the wee hours of the morning hadn't been replaced with a changeling of romantic dribble when I opened my laptop to the light of day. I'm never forsaking my genre again.

It's not until I'm in the elevator that I realize the person waiting is Darcy. With great effort I keep myself from banging my head against the reflective silver wall. Darcy takes in my frazzled appearance. He opens his mouth to say something, pauses, then bravely pushes ahead.

"I hear we're allies now," he says, looking forward rather than at me.

"We are," I say. "I'm your Joanna."

Darcy glances my way then and I give him my most predatory smile. His obvious confusion makes me sigh.

"You know, the girl from *The Hunger Games*?" I say. "She was allied with Katniss, but not because either of them wanted to be."

"I only saw the movie," Darcy admits. "And it was a long time ago."

"Oh, come on," I say. "You know Joanna from the movie. She was in the elevator dressed like a tree and then"

I stop mid-sentence as I remember what came next. I just likened myself to someone who stripped naked in an elevator while in an elevator with Darcy Delancey. He must have remembered the scene as well because he's blushing and staring straight ahead again.

"Please, don't," Darcy says under his breath.

I can't stop the tortured laugh that escapes my lips. Then Darcy is chuckling too and oh holy hobbits I like it. The pleasure rolling through me has to be from the brain fog and the lack of sleep and the break in tension, because it absolutely can not be about Darcy Delancey's laugh.

Darcy looks at me as the doors slide open. His gaze is warm, but also something more. We stay like that for long enough that the elevator pings and Darcy has to put his arm out to keep the doors from closing. The sound shakes me out of the trance and reminds me that I'm late to seminar.

And that I don't share moments with Darcy Delancey.

"I'll see you Friday night?" I ask, preparing for a quick exit.

"As long as you promise to keep your clothes on," Darcy says.

And with that he walks away, leaving me sputtering at his retreating back.

Darcy shows up Friday night with a giant bag of take-out. He's wearing a fitted black sweater and jeans, which may be the most casual outfit I've seen him in since we were toddling around in diapers. He looks good this way.

"Indian, as requested," he says, holding up the food like a proud dog with a dead squirrel. He looks too sincere to be faking.

"Stupid Andrew," I mumble under my breath.

"What's that?" Darcy asks.

"Nothing. C'mon in. Andrew and Olivia are doing something in the kitchen, but I'm sure they'll be out in a second."

As though on cue there's loud giggling from the other room. I give Darcy a "see what I have to put up with" look. He smirks. It may be my imagination, but I think he's also blushing.

Darcy follows me the ten steps from my front door to the table where I finish setting out plates and forks while he unpacks the bag. He takes out item after item, and I find myself fixating on his hands. They're strong with long fingers, and just the tiniest bit of hair. I've always thought of my own fingers as a little stubbier than they should be. His nails are trimmed and clean. What would that hand feel like on my cheek? Would the pads of those fingers be the slightest bit rough?

Wait. What? What in the . . ? Augh, stupid brain. Stupid Jane Austen. This is the kind of thing that drives the muses away.

"So, what's the plan?" Darcy asks.

"What?" My eyes fly to Darcy's face, terrified that he's somehow read my mind. But no. He looks no different than normal, except that now I'm thinking normal looks pretty hot. For the love of Gandalf, how do I turn this off?

Darcy's looking at me strangely now and I realize I never answered his question.

"We eat?" I say, as though it's a question.

"I meant for the alliance," Darcy says. "That is why we're here, right?"

"Right," I say. "Right. I mean, it's why you're here. I live here." Oh my gosh, Heather. You are not a rambler. Get it together. Back to something we know.

"I think we should pretend we hate each other," I say with all the confidence of a gaffer in the shire. "That way no one will suspect we're allies."

"That seems unnecessary," says Darcy. "The future dean will need to get along with everyone in the department in a professional manner."

"Fitzwilliam, do you ever stop being serious?" This feels better. A little needling. A little anger. I can work with this.

Darcy's frown is confused. "Aren't we here to discuss real strategy to keep Professors Pfisten and Arrington from becoming our evil overlords?"

"Wow, Heather," Olivia says as she carries a stack of glasses from the kitchen. "I think you're rubbing off on him. That sounds like the plot of one of your novels."

Thank God. Reinforcements have arrived.

"If only I could take them out with a dragon," I say with a smirk.

"I haven't come across any dragons in your writing yet," Darcy says.

Olivia looks from me to Darcy and back again.

"Excuse me?" she asks.

I can't stop my eye roll. "I let F.W. read one of my manuscripts, before I knew who he was."

"Who's F.W.?" Andrew asks. He's followed Olivia from the kitchen with a pitcher of something orange-colored and frothy.

"What's that?" I ask.

"Mango Lassi," he says. "Who's F.W.?"

"I am," says Darcy. "Heather and I were emailing each other as part of a writing contest."

"Cool," Andrew says. I'm grateful he's willing to leave it at that. "Try this and tell me what you think," he says.

Andrew pours the drinks into our cups, and he and Olivia join us at the table.

"Oh, my gosh," I say at first taste. "This is amazing. Olivia, you can never leave this man."

"Like I would," Olivia says, flashing Andrew a look that makes him grin.

"You know, Andrew," I say, "it fits the meal so well. It's almost like you knew Darcy would be bringing Indian food."

"Funny, that," Andrew says. "So where were we?"

"Heather thought they should pretend to hate each other, but Darcy thought that would be counter-productive," Olivia says. "That's as far as we've gotten."

"Hate is extreme," Darcy says. "But maybe we could pretend to annoy each other?"

I pause, a piece of sauce-soaked naan halfway to my mouth. "I don't know if I have that kind of acting skill," I say. Olivia snorts.

"You proposed this alliance," Darcy says.

"Actually, Olivia and Andrew did that. I agreed because it allows me to have coffee without interacting with Benji."

"And because of the evil overlords," Olivia chimes in.

"I'm surprised you want to try coffee again," Darcy says. "After Professer Pfisten's move last week."

158

"I'm not going to let that she-demon steal the joy of coffee from me. Not without a fight."

"Atta girl," Darcy says.

"What about Tweed?" Olivia asks. "Is he truly awful or just arrogant and entitled?"

"Tweed?" Darcy asks.

"Professor Randal," Andrew says.

"Ah."

"You can be arrogant and entitled without being truly awful," I say with a pointed look at Darcy.

"Hey," he says, sounding truly hurt.

"I meant it as a compliment," I say, smirking. I'm aware that I'm leaning pretty hard into this antagonism, but I have to if I'm going to retain my sanity, what with the unwelcome tingles at cornhole and the frequent gifts of coffee. "Anyway, Tweed would be the worst to work under. Doesn't he strike you as the kind of guy who'd take credit for your ideas and then make you do all the work?"

"He's actually done that to me," Andrew says.

"Really?" Darcy asks. "When did you work with Arrington?

"It was my second year here, and I was on a cross-disciplinary committee for the enhancement of something or other. Arrington acted like he'd been tasked to run the thing, which I later found out wasn't the case. He delegated everything out and then took credit when the idea was chosen for implementation."

"What a jerk," Olivia says.

"It was a one-off, so I got over it," Andrew replies. "But working under a guy like that full-time would be a nightmare."

Darcy and I look at each other.

"Brainstorming: Go," I say.

"How about we compliment each other's strengths at the interviews?" Darcy asks.

"I'd have done that anyway," I say.

"Really?"

"I'm only mean to your face, Fitzwilliam," I say. "I actually like you ok when you're not around."

"Kind of like how you like me outside of Kansas City," Andrew says to Olivia.

"I like you fine everywhere now," she replies.

I roll my eyes.

"Is it going to be like this all night?" Darcy asks.

"It'll get worse," I say. "What can you two actually contribute to this alliance?" I ask the lovebirds.

"We got the ball rolling," Andrew says.

"And we're here to cool things down if it gets heated," Olivia says.

"Says the girl who landed Andrew on his butt two weeks ago?" I ask.

"Not the kind of heated I was referring to," she says.

I roll my eyes, but my traitorous cheeks are burning. I don't let myself look at Darcy.

"Then your presence here is unnecessary," Darcy says.

Not gonna lie, it stings just a little to hear him dismiss the idea of any heat between us so casually.

"Why don't you two go do whatever it is you do on Friday night?" Darcy continues.

Now it's Andrew blushing. Isn't that cute.

"C'mon," Olivia says, standing and reaching a hand to Andrew. "It's clear we're not wanted."

As they leave the room he says something too low for me to hear and Olivia giggles.

"Are they always like that?" Darcy asks.

"Always."

"Maybe next time we meet at my place," he says.

"Let's do this right so we don't need a next time."

"Fine," Darcy nods. "Brainstorming, commence."

We don't fight through the whole session. In fact, we act like reasonable adult humans, assuming reasonable adult humans would be plotting an alliance in the pursuit of a promotion.

It's really very pleasant. Not that I'm willing to admit that out loud when Olivia asks me later that night after the guys have gone.

Tattoo 6: Eagle in Flight

When I told my mom I wanted to get a tattoo for my dad she said "Oh, Heather." But then she helped me brainstorm. I learned as much about my mom as I did my dad that day. So I suppose this tattoo is hers as much as it's his.

"He'd rock you for hours," Mom told me. "From the very beginning, you'd always stopped crying when he held you. At first it was a joke. 'What will I do if you're not here?' And then it wasn't funny anymore. Near the end, when he could barely move the chair, he'd still hold you. I begged him not to leave me, but he smiled down into your face and promised he was leaving the best of himself behind."

I wonder sometimes who I'd be if I'd been raised by that man. Never distant. Never angry.

I know it's not fair to compare my step-dad to a memory, but sometimes I can't help it. Most times I can't help it.

Anyway, I chose an eagle. I was thinking dragon, but in Tolkien they're always the bad guys. The eagles are the heroes, the wise ones. The rescuers.

My dad's tattoo is small, the outline of an eagle in flight, placed behind my ear with the date he died. I don't see it unless I look for it, but I know it's there. Like him. Somewhere.

Chapter 36

When Titans Collide

"I nearly can't bring her out in public, it's so bad," says Professor Timothy Arrington III. "She's really let herself go."

The look I give Darcy isn't subtle. It very clearly says *shut him up, or I will murder him, and prison will end the practicality of our alliance.* Before Darcy can speak, the not-sexy librarian takes Tweed's correction into her own capable hands.

"Timothy," she says, "I'm hearing some latent self-congratulations in your voice, perhaps due to an opinion that you've maintained your own body in a better state. The best thinkers are currently agreed that a woman's physical attractiveness is generally in direct proportion to her satisfaction in sexual encounters. Are you telling us that you're selfish in bed?"

She just said that? I can't contain my laugh, a short guffaw that I attempt to cover with a cough.

Tweed is sputtering, unable to form words.

"Well, then, productive meeting, team," Darcy says. "Let's table this until next week. You all know what you need to accomplish before then."

Timothy shoves his phone in his pocket and picks up the briefcase he'd never unpacked. He's out the door in moments.

"Hopefully he's going to attend to his wife's appearance," Professor Pfisten says as she calmly gathers her things and follows him.

I can't look at Darcy. I tell myself it's because I'll start laughing, but there's also a self-consciousness I'm unwilling to examine.

"Well, that was interesting," Darcy says when Pfisten leaves the room. "I'd tell you you're looking lovely today, but now I'm afraid of the implications."

My eyes shoot up. I can't help it. He stands there, smirking, then seems to realize what he said.

"Oh, my gosh. I'm sorry. I didn't think that through." Darcy has run his hands through his hair and looked away. He looks back. "I'm never complimenting a woman on her appearance again."

And I can't help it. Now I do laugh, just to put him out of his misery.

"We nearly don't need an alliance, with those two working so hard against each other," I say.

"Yes, but if one leaves the field, the other will turn upon us. I think that's Pfisten's strategy, anyway. To take us out one at a time."

"Did she think I'd run after the coffee?" I ask.

"Maybe. She was probably testing your metal, so to speak."

Darcy and I are walking towards the parking lot, chatting, as though it were normal. It's a gorgeous fall day, with all the smells of drying leaves and crisp but not too cold air. I can even pick up a bit of distant bonfire if I try, although it may just be my imagination.

"Fall has always been my favorite season," I say. "I missed it when I was in L.A. for undergrad."

165

"Is that why you came back?" he asks. "The seasons?"

"No. My Mima wasn't doing well. I didn't want to lose the time she had left."

"I'm sorry to hear that," he says.

"I got two years with her during my mba, and I wouldn't give those up for anything," I say. "She's why I have that butterfly tattoo on my shoulder."

"You mentioned that," Darcy says. Am I imagining it, or did his eyes just get darker? We walk on in a silence that is just shy of companionable.

"So why did you end up coming to Kansas City?" I ask.

"Actually," he says, "your step-dad got me the job."

"Harry? Really?"

"Yeah. Our mothers were involved, I'm sure. But Harry has quite a bit of pull with the board."

"He should," I say, "with the amount of money his family has given over the generations. I'm surprised there isn't a hall named after them."

"I'm surprised I didn't think, even back then, that he might do the same for you," Darcy says. "Truly, I am sorry that I wasn't aware of who you were."

"Would it have made a difference?" I ask.

"Certainly."

"Why?"

"Why what?"

"Why would it have made a difference?" I ask. "It's not like it would have changed who either of us was as a person."

"I don't know, Heather," Darcy says with the smallest hint of irritation. "But it's human, isn't it? To have a sense of closeness to those you have commonality with? I mean, our mothers have been best friends forever. We played together as babies."

"You stole my basket," I say, with a mock glare.

He holds up his hands. "I yield," he says, laughing. "The basket is yours."

We've reached the staff lot and are standing beside my civic. My stomach growls.

"Do you want to grab something to eat?" I ask without thinking. Darcy's face grows instantly uncomfortable. Shoot.

"Actually," he says, " I have an, er, appointment."

"A dinner appointment?" I ask, and then it dawns on me. "You have a date," I say with a big grin. I actually reach out and poke him with my finger. What am I doing?

"Well, yes. Of sorts."

"You move quick, don't you? We haven't even been broken up for three weeks yet!"

"Heather, we were never actually dating," Darcy says.

"Technicality," I say, rolling my eyes. "So who is she?" I'm trying to keep this cool. Slightly mocking, almost. I don't care if Darcy has a date. Of course I don't.

"She's from the app. My mother set it up."

"The app that matches you by credit score?" I ask.

"I should never have told you about that."

"Probably not," I say with a shrug and a Cheshire cat grin. "Well, I bet she has a lovely 401k."

Darcy sighs. "I'm sure she does, although that's not what my mother is filtering for."

I raise an eyebrow expectantly, but Darcy doesn't continue. And you know what, I really don't want to know. Because that would mean I cared, which I don't.

"You know," I say, "Olivia had some words for Andrew about the kind of man who lets his mother choose who he dates."

"My own choices haven't worked out well recently," he says, and I can't help but wonder if he means me or someone else. "Regardless, I need to get going if I don't want to be late."

He looks at me like I might argue. What does he expect, that I'll beg him to cancel his date and hang out with me instead? No thank you.

When I don't say anything he nods once and turns towards his nice shiny Tesla. I watch him. It's safe, with his back towards me. Right before he gets in he looks back and catches me staring. Shoot.

"Hey, Darcy," I call, just to cover.

"Yes?"

"Can you bring me a coffee tomorrow? I'll pay in gold."

"Sure," he says. He smiles, this one small, lips tight together, and gets into his car. Why is it that, as he drives away, I feel like something's been lost?

Chapter 37

HR and other necessary hurdles

When I get home Olivia and Andrew are playing a board game at the kitchen table. I take my drive thru salad to the couch and click on Hulu. Forty five minutes later, after Olivia's decisive victory and longer than necessary for a standard goodbye spent on the front porch, Andrew leaves.

Olivia comes back in with a goofy expression and plops down on the couch.

"How was the meeting?" she asks.

"Meh."

Olivia raises an eyebrow.

"It is what you'd expect. Tweed and the Librarian sniping at each other. There's no love lost there."

"Is there love anywhere else?" Olivia asks.

"No," I say, squirming slightly. "Definitely not. In fact, when I left him Darcy was headed to a date."

"Really?" Olivia looks genuinely confused.

"Yeah, really," I say. "That's not so surprising. He's objectively a good catch, if you're into uptight trust fund professors with Jane Austen obsessions."

"Oh, yeah, " Olivia says. "It's hard to find anyone who'd want a rich, intelligent, gentlemanly sort. Much better a barista with a nose ring."

Well, when you put it that way . . .

"Regardless," I say, "I wish Darcy the best of luck on his date. May they marry and have many tiny Fitzwilliams and Elizabeths."

"Okay . . ." Says Olivia, stretching out the word. "So when do your interviews start? For the dean position?"

"My first is tomorrow."

"Tomorrow?!?" This time Olivia squeals. "How have you not told me? What are you wearing."

I shrug.

"Do you seriously not care about this at all?" Olivia asks.

"Not really."

"What will you do if they choose you?"

"I can't imagine they'd be that irresponsible." I've wandered to the kitchen and am opening cabinets. Surely Olivia has stashed something sweet in here. She comes up behind me, pulls a box of golden Oreos out from the back of a bottom shelf and hands it to me.

"So, just to make sure I understand, you don't want the dean position, and you honestly don't want to date Darcy. Correct?"

"Correct." I say it with no hesitation, mainly because Olivia is a pit bull with romance of any kind. If her jaw clamps, it's not releasing.

"That's just as well," she says. "You couldn't date if either of you was the boss anyway."

I'm pouring myself a glass of almond milk, my first Oreo already in my mouth. "What do you mean?" I ask around it.

"That's an HR thing, right?" Olivia says, reaching for a cookie in the tray. "They don't love it if you date a colleague, but it's not an actual issue unless there are lines of authority involved."

I hadn't thought of that. And even though I don't want the job, I don't want Tweed or Pfisten to get it. Which leaves Darcy.

It's a good thing I don't like him. Or, I mean, fine. I like him. He's a nice guy. But it's a good thing I don't like him like that.

Chapter 38

Victorian Propriety

Tittering?

Why is there tittering in my Advanced Culture and Cognition classroom?

I look towards the sound, two young women seated near the back, and then past them to where Darcy Delancey stands by the door of the half-filled auditorium. Professional me manages to suppress my eye roll, but on the inside those marbles are spinning.

"Last question," I say. "Who's got a good one?"

A suck-up in the front row asks something insightful, and I redirect it to my students who bounce around several good suggestions before getting to the answer I would have given. Well played, class. I dismiss them with a reminder to study for Thursday's test then gather my laptop and notes.

Springvale is a small university, and the college of humanities is smaller still, so I'm unsurprised by how many people greet Darcy on their way out. I follow the stream of students up the stairs. As I reach Darcy, he lifts two paper cups and one eyebrow. A bag dangles from his wrist.

"Is this my coffee?" I ask.

"No. I thought I'd change things up and get you a matcha today."

Whatever look is on my face causes Darcy to laugh, and I'm annoyed by how much I enjoy the sound.

"Joking!" he says. "Just joking! Here."

He shoves a cup into my waiting hand. I look from it to Darcy and back again before taking a hesitant sip. Oh, coffee glory. My shoulders ease.

"Don't joke about coffee," I say. But when I look up again, Darcy's watching my mouth.

"Hey," I say. His eyes dart to mine.

"Don't joke about coffee."

He smiles. "Never again."

I walk with Darcy from the always slightly chilly and dim building where all of the humanities seminars are held into bright October sunshine.

"I thought we could have lunch at the picnic tables behind Barnum Hall," Darcy says, indicating the bag he's holding. "It's a great day out."

With the settling in of the semester completed and midterms not yet looming, this is the perfect time to enjoy Autumn. I tell myself this is why I go along with Darcy's plan without argument. We talk about the students he knew from my class, Darcy referencing names and in a couple of cases notable papers they'd done two or three years ago.

"I don't know how you do that," I say. "I'm lucky to know a student's name when I've had her three semesters in a row."

Darcy shrugs. "Just a gift, I suppose," he says. It's not, though. It's a direct result of how Darcy cares about other people. I don't examine what this says about me.

"Is this good?" Darcy asks.

There are two empty picnic tables, one in sun and one in shade. Darcy stands beside the sunny one, and for once I don't fight him.

"Perfect," I say, taking a seat.

Darcy unloads two sandwiches and a package of kettle chips from his bag, placing them on the table before us.

"Are you bribing me right now?" I ask. "Because I already had my first interview. It's too late to change what I said."

Darcy's grin is genuine, that slightly-turned incisor exposed. I distract myself by reading the labels on the sandwiches. Chicken avocado BLT or Grilled Gruyere and tomato. How to choose?

"No bribery," Darcy says. "We didn't get to eat last night, so I figured I'd make up for it."

"That's right," I say. "How was your date?" I don't look up from the sandwiches.

"It was fine. The most memorable part of the night was the proposal happening at the table beside ours. That was a bit awkward on a first date."

"It would have been even more awkward if you'd been together a while and were dragging your feet," I say.

"Indeed," Darcy says. "Which sandwich do you want?"

"They aren't both for me?" Darcy's used to this by now, and gives no reply other than a huff of breath. "Here," I say, passing him the chicken avocado. "I don't think you'd be the 'dragging your feet' type, anyway."

"Really?" This surprises him. "My mother would say otherwise."

"Foot-dragging goes against your Victorian sense of propriety," I say, taking a first delicious bite of my sandwich.

"Georgian," Darcy corrects on auto-pilot and then seems to choke on a chip as he coughs out "Wait, no."

I barely manage to swallow before my laugh bursts free. "Fitzwilliam, are you attempting to tell me you've turned to a life of debauchery, because I won't believe it. Your morality is Victorian to the core. I bet you asked your date's permission before you gave her a chaste kiss goodnight."

I ignore the hollowness in my stomach at the thought and take another bite of my sandwich.

"I didn't kiss her goodnight," Darcy says while concentrating on removing his tomato. "She was very sweet, but I don't see a future there. We ended the evening amicably with a hand shake and no illusions."

The sandwich must be doing its job because the hollowness is gone. I finish chewing before I speak, one lesson my mother taught me that I've retained. Because see-food is gross.

"You've proven my point." I say. "A true Georgian would have taken that kiss regardless."

"I wasn't practicing restraint," Darcy says. "I didn't want to kiss her." He looks up from his sandwich and his eyes are darker somehow. Can blue eyes smolder? "Heather," he says. But he doesn't continue. Just keeps looking at me.

"Are you about to ask to kiss *me*, Fitzwilliam?"

I don't know why I say it. In the uncomfortable moment, it just pops out, and now it's there, hanging between us.

"Would you say 'yes' if I did?"

Would I? Will I?

No, of course not. Maybe?

"Professor Delancey? Is that you?"

The spell is broken by a chirpy voice. I pull my gaze away from Darcy's to see a student, complete with requisite backpack and straightened pony-tail, coming our way. These tables are tucked into a courtyard at the back of a cluster of buildings. They're generally ignored by students and staff alike, but Darcy's groupies will find him anywhere. I swear, it's like dating a celebrity.

If we were dating.

"Hello, Samantha," Darcy says, his smile tight. "Is there something I can help you with?

To her credit, Samantha looks at me and seems to realize she's interrupted something. "Oh, no, not really," she says. "I was just surprised to see you, you know, out and about."

"Like seeing your dentist at a Taylor Swift concert?" I ask.

"Yeah," she giggles. "Exactly like that." She stands there for a moment longer. Is she hoping we'll invite her to sit? Because as much as I don't want to resume our previous conversation, that won't be happening. "Well, then, I'll just go" Samantha says. "See you in seminar."

"See you there." Darcy nods and smiles his professorly smile as Samantha adjusts her backpack and goes on her way.

"Well, then," Darcy says.

"Yeah," I say. "You're a popular man."

"Only with some." Darcy's gaze is back on me, and his question still lingers.

"I think there'd be HR issues," I say on a rush, before his beautiful blues can suck me back in. "If you were to, well, you know. Kiss me."

Oh my gosh, could I be any more awkward? I'm worse than a groupie. Get it together, Heather.

"HR issues?" Darcy asks.

I look down and realize I've been creasing and re-creasing my sandwich wrapper. I'm practically doing origami over here. I take a deep breath and continue.

"If one of us were to be Dean, which I think we both agree is a better outcome than working for Pfisten or Tweed, us dating would be a problem. There'd be lines of authority to consider."

"Ah. I see." Darcy pauses. "And if there weren't? HR issues, that is?"

Why won't he just let this drop? I swear, even when I really hated him, it wasn't because he was pushy.

"We tried dating for one night and ended up in a fight and broken up by the end of the evening," I say, desperate now not to answer his question. Either to him or to myself.

"But that was staged," Darcy says. "That was the plan."

"It was a good plan," I say, although I'm not sure of that any more. Is it still a good plan? Because from here, with the picnic and coffee and sunshine, his lips are looking rather kissable.

No, Heather. Just, no.

Darcy, who can usually read me better than anyone besides Olivia, doesn't pick up on my wavering. He leans his shoulders back and nods.

"I see," Darcy says. "Then I suppose it's good it worked out as it has. This way we can continue as colleagues without any pesky HR issues in the way."

"Exactly," I say.

He clearly doesn't believe it, but he forces a smile and so do I. We somehow manage to transition into a conversation about our interviews thus far. The sun isn't shining quite as brightly, and the breeze feels colder, but its better this way.

Chapter 39

Mine is bigger

I manage not to see Darcy until our next Monday meeting. I hear him occasionally, with his groupies, but I keep my door closed. Inside my cave, I eat Oreos and caffeinate with juice-based energy drinks instead of glorious lattes. I tell myself I like it this way.

Despite arriving fifteen minutes early to the meeting Monday, I'm still the last one here. Darcy's smile is genuine, if reserved. The not-sexy librarian doesn't roll her eyes, but it's close. "Good, we can finally begin," she says. I let it run off my back like coffee off a table's edge. Because I'm just that evolved.

Tweed hasn't bothered to look up from his phone, but as I seat myself at the table he finally places it face-down on the surface and looks to Darcy who, if we're honest, has become the defacto leader.

"So what are we covering today, Delancey?" he asks.

"And why would he be in charge of that?" Pfisten says.

"No reason," Tweed replies, a little too casually. Is he doing this on purpose? Pitting Pfisten against Darcy? If anyone in this room is going to have animosity towards Darcy, it's going to be me, thank you.

"Professor Pfisten could lead instead," I say. "But someone needs to. We're two weeks out from the presentation, and we need to get things done."

The look Darcy shoots me is a little confused, but he doesn't argue. Pfisten needs no further encouragement. She delegates like a general with little need for or attention to outside input.

I couldn't care less, as long as we don't look like fools at the retirement party, and Darcy has always been a team player, which leaves Tweed as the only hold-out. They bicker back and forth, but ultimately Tweed doesn't care any more than I do. If what Andrew says is true, and I have no reason to doubt him, Tweed's planning on having his TAs do his part anyway.

"A very productive meeting," Pfisten says. "Look, we're ending right on time. Doesn't that bode well for the future?"

I'm not sure if she asks it as a hypothetical, but no one replies as we gather our things.

"Want to stop by Shenanigans for a drink before heading home?" Tweed asks Darcy.

I don't know what Tweed's game is, as to the best of my knowledge they've never hung out before, but Darcy isn't playing.

"I'm sorry, Timothy. I can't." My heart warms just a little bit. Despite the awkwardness between us, Darcy's a one-alliance man.

"Come on," Tweed pushes. "Just a quick shot. I'm buying."

"Actually," Darcy pulls at his collar. He's not glancing my way. "I have other plans."

Ah. Just like he had other plans last Monday. Apparently Mondays are date night and our picnic meant nothing. Or maybe, after I've rejected him twice he wants to prove he's not pining for me. Or maybe it's not a date at all. He could be playing cornhole or adopting a puppy or something.

Tweed nudges Darcy with an elbow. "Big plans on a Monday night?" he asks. "The kind of plans a Bachelor looks forward to? Man, I'm living through you, brother."

Ew. Just ew. Darcy looks as uncomfortable as I feel.

"Well, then, I must be off," Darcy says. "Good evening, ladies."

Pfisten doesn't look up from her laptop, just lifts a hand in Darcy's direction. I force my lips to form a smile.

"Have a nice night," I say.

He smiles back, lips closed, nods, and is gone.

"Wish I were him tonight," Tweed says, staring at the door Darcy left through.

"You were never him," Pfisten says.

I couldn't agree more.

Chapter 40

Rich Dog, Poor Dog

I'm scrolling on the couch, waiting on Olivia to finish showering so we can watch "Penelope" for the umpteenth time.

As you might imagine, I've been a bit more obsessed with Ash since he announced his engagement. This might be because I was so involved last time around, or maybe it's because his fiancé, Zoe, has enough followers that she didn't notice when I subscribed, allowing me a whole new view of my brother's life, if only peripherally.

Most likely it's because the engagement has brought up a million questions. Who is this girl? How did they meet? And, now that I can tell she's an absolutely amazing person with no interest in anything materialistic or vaguely classist, how in the world did they end up together?

Don't get me wrong. I can imagine anyone falling in love with Ash. He's my baby brother and entirely loveable. But if I'm honest, the man he became under the influence of his former best friend and our father, well, I probably wouldn't like that man much if I were to meet him without context. And from what I've been able to glean from the fake account with Olivia's picture that I use to follow his socials now, he only became worse after the wedding fell through. More concerned with promotion and appearances and status.

Zoe gives me hope that the little brother I knew is still in there somewhere.

I can't ask Mom my questions. It makes her uncomfortable because she never knows how much she's allowed to tell me, and that makes both of us sad. So, I scroll.

While Ash's posts are sporadic, generally photos he's tagged in at fancy galas and pseudo-profound quotes about success, Zoe's accounts are dedicated to finding homes for the dogs and cats at the shelter she works for in downtown Denver. Her feed is filled with pictures of animals, stats about adoption and the importance of getting pets spayed or neutered.

Tonight I find a link to an account titled "Rich Dog, Poor Dog." In the top post, a chihuahua and a corgi trot along at the end of their leashes. A voice from off camera, one I recognize as Zoe from other videos, says "Who are my good puppies?" At the sound both dogs look over a shoulder, happy tongues lolling from their mouths. Zoe laughs.

It's no wonder Ash loves her.

Below in the comments, people make their guesses. Which is the rich dog, which the poor? The mystery will be solved next time when the dog available for adoption is revealed.

"What's that?" Olivia asks, plopping down beside me on the couch. She's in pjs, hair still wet from the shower. I hand her my phone.

"Oh my gosh, they're so cute," Olivia coos.

"Aren't they?"

"Which is which?" Olivia asks.

"No clue," I shrug. "And I think that's the point she's making."

"Wait," Olivia says. "Is this Zoe? Your soon-to-be sister in law?"

"Yeah," I say. "It's cool, isn't it? How she's creating social commentary with dogs?"

"She's smart and a good person," Olivia says. "Why is she marrying your brother?"

I take my phone back without answering. There's no reason to defend him yet again. Olivia's dislike of Ash goes deep. She was with me right after the wedding fail. She inhabited my Covid bubble when the tears were constant, and so was the checking to see if I'd been unblocked on any of his socials. Olivia has tried multiple times to convince me that, while what I did was horrible (you know it's bad when even Olivia admits that), Ash still needs to forgive me. He's family. The longer Ash goes without forgiving me, the more firmly set Olivia's resentment becomes.

To be fair, she has none of the tempering love or guilt I experience. I'm sure I'd feel the same way if someone treated her this badly.

"I'm making brownies," Olivia says, rising from the couch. "It'll just take a minute to get them in the oven."

I stare at my phone, go again to Zoe's homepage. I would love to know this woman some day.

"Come help me," Olivia calls from the kitchen. I do. Better to enjoy the amazing people that want me in their lives than to pine for those who don't.

Chapter 41

Dating Janes

It's the last meeting before Dean Mitchell's retirement party, and Tweed didn't even bother to show. He sent an email saying he'd see us Saturday and attached his portion of the presentation. The three of us watch it together on Darcy's laptop. It's not bad at all.

"I bet he had a TA do it," the Not-Sexy Librarian says with a scowl.

I can't help but agree. There's no way a man whose technological savvy has thus far been limited to cat videos could have created this. But I don't care. It covers what he was delegated and fits the overall theme. It could have been made by a mountain troll and it wouldn't matter to me.

When the official meeting ends, Pfisten pulls me into a subtext-heavy sidebar conversation about how this department will run once *the new Dean* is in place. I expect Darcy to be gone by the time I reach the lobby, but he's still there, chatting with a willowy blond. She's leaning in, smiling. A very pretty smile. He gestures towards the hallway with the restrooms, and she reaches out and squeezes his forearm before walking purposely in that direction. He watches her go.

"Another Jane?" I ask, coming up beside him.

Darcy looks from her retreating form to me. "What?"

"Is she a new Jane or the one from last week?" I ask. "Does she teach kindergarten at a school for the deaf?"

"Actually, she's in finance," Darcy says, looking down at me with that quizzical expression of his. "She was the person I met last week though. Her name is Meredith. Why did you call her 'Jane'?"

"You have a type."

"A type?"

"Yes. Pretty. Sweet. Kind. A 'Jane.'" I say.

"By your definition, a 'Jane' is most men's type," Darcy says. I have only a moment to feel the sting before he continues. "As you might guess, however, I am more an 'Elizabeth' man."

The way he's looking at me . . . Does he see me as an 'Elizabeth'?

I break eye contact and glance towards the ladies room.

"Then maybe you should stop dating Janes," I say. "Their hearts are fragile."

The woman is returning now, all sweet smiles. Darcy introduces me and I wish them a wonderful evening. Of course, it's a lie.

Chapter 42

Halloween

Halloween snuck up on me this year. Olivia, who goes absolutely bonkers for this day, has always handled the costume aspect for us both. I had one rule: no overalls. As long as she stuck to that, she had free reign.

We've been Lilo and Stitch, Donkey and Shrek, Simon and Garfunkel (that one took some explaining). My favorite was Alice and the Queen of Hearts. Olivia even let me carry a bloody ax that time. Not a real one, of course.

But here's the thing . . . I know my best friend. And I knew that her suggestion we go as Mario and Luigi, brought up every year with a "just kidding" attached, wasn't a joke. It was a heart's desire. This year when she asked how I'd feel about bringing Andrew into our costuming plans I bailed out gracefully rather than ending up dressed as Princess Peach.

Fast forward to me, less than an hour before we're supposed to leave for the annual Halloween Monster Bash at Fiona's. I'm standing in front of my closet trying to cobble together a costume that doesn't look so last minute that Olivia feels guilty all night for abandoning me to my own devices. My eye catches on my hatbox of scarves (yeah, that's a thing in my closet), and inspiration strikes.

I leave my room a smarmy but remarkable pirate. This probably isn't surprising, considering my general fashion leanings. I don't own overalls, but a corset and hoop earrings? Yeah, got those. The tattoos don't hurt the cause either.

"All right, people. It's time to walk the plank," I say as I stride down the hall in my black knee-high boots. I've taken to announcing my entrances so I don't have to see the kissing.

Andrew and Olivia are in the kitchen. They look adorable as Mario and Luigi in their fake mustaches and little caps.

"You're going as a pirate?" Andrew asks.

"Does this surprise you?" I counter.

"It's just that" Andrew stops mid-sentence and glances down at Olivia. Did she pinch him?

"You look great, Heather," Olivia says. "We'd better get going. Fiona's will be packed."

Olivia is, of course, correct in this prediction. Fi's Place is wall to wall people. The "No Shirts, No Service" rule has been suspended for the night, and more than one set of sexy Aladdin abs are showing. There are also the obligatory Barbie outfits, Vampires, and a disturbing number of Deadpool costumes.

"Look at you," a familiar voice says as I follow Olivia and Andrew towards a table in the back.

I turn to see Benji. He's clearly supposed to be Aquaman, with his leather pants, armguards and broomstick trident. He's shirtless and black swirls made to look like scales or tattoos cover his chest and shoulders. His grin tells me he's well aware that his bare self is worth showing off.

"Benji, nice to see so much of you," I say with a smirk.

"You haven't been by the Cranky Bean lately." Benji leans in to be heard over the music and general hum of people. Or maybe just to be closer.

"No, I've been scaling back my caffeine intake," I say. Benji doesn't need to know it's because I'm avoiding him.

"That's too bad," he says. "I've missed you."

I roll my eyes. "I'm sure you've survived," I say. Benji grins.

"I'm counting down the months until graduation," he says. "What do you say, maybe Halloween can be a free pass?"

"A free pass to do what, Benji?" I ask

His grin grows even bigger and he shrugs, making his painted muscles flex. "Anything we want."

Am I tempted? Looking at Benji I realize he's exactly what twenty-two year old me would have found sexy beyond endurance. He would have been how old when I was twenty-two? (Don't do the math, Heather!) Regardless, now I'm just not interested.

"Sorry, Benji," I say with a shake of my head. "It isn't going to happen."

"It was worth a shot," Benji says with one last grin. I watch him merge back into the crowd, for the briefest moment wondering if that paint would smear beneath my fingers . . .

"Persistent one, our Benji."

The sound of a voice, *his* voice, so close to my ear makes me start. I turn to find Darcy directly behind me, protectively holding two glasses.

"Don't want these to spill," he says. "The bar is packed." Which is Darcy's nice way of saying that if I can't keep from knocking these out of his hands, it's going to be half an hour before we can get more drinks.

"Would you like the 'Witch's Brew' or the 'Vampire Kiss'?" he asks.

I glance at his outfit to make sure he's not Dracula before answering and realize, no. Just no.

"You're a pirate," I say.

"You're observant," he replies. "And a pirate as well."

"I'm going to kill Olivia," I say. Darcy raises an eyebrow, so I explain. "She knew I'd change if I realized we were dressed alike, so she stopped Andrew from telling me."

"Ah," Darcy says. "Well, I'm glad she did. You make a lovely pirate."

I roll my eyes. "'Lovely,' Darcy? That's the best adjective you could find for this outfit?" I gesture with one hand towards the black leather encasing me. Darcy's eyes follow my gesture appreciatively. Is it hot in here?

"Just give me the 'Vampire Kiss,'" I say.

And did I imagine it, or did his eyes skip to my lips?

I'm feeling bold as I take the drink from his hand. Dressing as a pirate will do that to a girl. I raise the cup to my mouth and take a sip. Not bad. Kind of like Cherry Coke and Vodka had a baby. Darcy, on the other hand, is grimacing into his cup.

"Not a fan of 'Witch's Brew'?" I ask.

"Apparently not," he says. "It tastes like a green warhead."

"Really?"

Without thinking, I take the drink from Darcy's hand and taste it. It's rather good, actually.

"Here you go," I say, giving him the Vampire Kiss. "See if you like this any better."

He looks from the drink to me and back like he's mulling it over.

"What, Fitzwilliam, do you think I have cooties?"

He frowns. "It's not that."

"You drank after me before," I say. "At the restaurant with our mothers."

"Yes, but we were dating then," he says. "It would have looked strange if I'd refused."

I roll my eyes. "Fine," I say. "Give it back."

I try to take the cup but he holds it away. I follow, reaching to grab it, then realize how close together this has brought us. I'm not pressed against him, but close. And the heels of my boots are so delightfully tall. His mouth is right there, closer than it's ever been.

Screw it. This is Halloween. I'm taking my pass.

Chapter 43

The Pass

I am in the middle of a crowded bar, dressed like a pirate, kissing Darcy Delancey.

And I like it.

Darcy must like it too, because the hand that isn't holding a drink is now on the small of my back. He's drawn me in closer and his lips taste tangy like sour warheads and insanity and what am I doing?

I pull back, blinking. Darcy's eyes open and gaze into mine.

"Well, then," he says.

"I, I'm sorry," I stammer. "I don't know what, I mean, uh, yeah." Articulate. That's me.

Darcy smiles. "I'd rather you not apologize for that, really," he says. "Although it may complicate things."

"Wait, no," I say. "No complicating. It's Halloween. It's just a pass. I am not working for Tweed."

Darcy chuckles. "No one wants that. But what do you mean 'a pass?'"

"It's Halloween," I say. "I'm not me. I'm a pirate. And, obviously, so are you." I make a gesture between us. "We're not us tonight. So we get a pass."

Darcy looks like he's contemplating this, and I'm sure his aforementioned Victorian morality is going to win out, but then his eyes darken. "If we're taking a pass, we're doing it right. Come with me."

He takes my drink from my hand and puts both the Vampire Kiss and the Witch's Brew in a nearby bus tub. Then my hand is in Darcy's and he's pulled me out the front door of Fiona's and around the side to a small parking lot. I barely have time to contemplate what Darcy means by "doing it right" when my back is against the brick wall, his hands cupping my face. His pirate's hat casts his eyes in shadow, so I reach up and pull it off. The gaze I reveal is dark. Heated. So not Darcy Delancey as I've known him.

And then his mouth is on mine, and he's devouring me. And I love being devoured. Suddenly I can't get enough of the taste of him or the feel of him. My hands are on his back and it's as firm as I remember.

"Heather," Darcy says against my lips, his voice raspy.

"Shhh," I say. "No names tonight."

He pauses, pulls back.

"But it's you I'm kissing," he says. "It's you I want to kiss."

I draw him to me, take his mouth with mine all the while blessing the heels of my boots that make his lips so very accessible.

"Get a room," someone hollers, and I realize there's warm skin beneath my fingertips. When did my hands make their way beneath his shirt? I pull them away, lift them out to the side so I'm not touching him with anything but my mouth. Darcy notices. Reaches out and

193

intertwines his fingers with mine. The kiss doesn't stop. It's somehow more intimate than my hands on his back.

Eventually Darcy's mouth slows against my lips. He begins to pull away and I catch his lower lip in my teeth. I can feel his smile form, and I don't want to let go. But I do with a sound of protest that makes Darcy chuckle.

He lets go of my hands and pulls me into him, nuzzling his face into my hair. I can't help it. I wrap my arms around him.

His smell is clean and spicy as I breathe him in. I'm standing here, holding and being held by Darcy Delancey and it doesn't feel like a pass. It feels like . . . no. I can't go there. Won't go there. I'll just stand for a few more moments and be held.

"Heather," Darcy says, sometime or no time later. He pulls back, puts his hands up to cup my face again. Traces my cheekbones with his thumbs and looks into my eyes. Captures me so I can't look away.

He's about to be serious. To want to talk and dissect and define, and I can't do that. He must see it. How is it he knows me this well?

He places a kiss lightly on my forehead. "Let's go inside," he says. "Andrew and Olivia must wonder where we are."

He doesn't try to take my hand as we walk back around the corner to the door and enter Fiona's. I'm glad. I wouldn't have let him. Our pass is over.

I excuse myself to the bathroom as soon as we get inside and give my mirror self a firm talking to about how we're going to handle the rest of the evening. I swear she rolls her eyes.

When I join Olivia and Andrew at their table, the remaining seat is, of course, next to Darcy. Do I feel his gaze more often tonight or is that my imagination causing heat to rise to my cheeks? The room is too loud for conversation, even with Darcy sitting right beside me. If my leg brushes against his, and if I don't move it away, surely that's the forced proximity of the crowd. Or maybe blame the Witch's Brew. It's so easy to allow yourself to be lost, to be not yourself, in a room full of disguises. In a room where reality has blurred, just for tonight.

One of the best things about Fiona's is that it's walking distance to our bungalow. No need for Ubers or a designated driver. The world is pleasantly fuzzy around the edges by the time we leave.

Andrew is walking us home, of course, but Darcy lives in the opposite direction. The four of us stand in front of Fiona's, just twenty feet from that parking lot. That wall.

Darcy holds his pirate hat in one hand. His hair is still perfect despite being covered most of the night. It's calling me to run my fingers through it. To muss it up. But if I do, I may not stop there. I don't know what he sees on my face, but his look darkens, so reminiscent of before, right before he took my mouth . . .

"Hey, this way you two!" Olivia's voice. How did I forget she's standing right here? Darcy and his stupid piratical magnetism. Really, it has to be the costume.

I tear my eyes from Darcy's gaze and look towards Olivia. She's holding her phone up to take a picture. Looking at the screen, she frowns. "Get closer," she says. My bossy little friend. We obey. Darcy stands right behind my shoulder now, and I feel the heat of him along my body. Surely this is all my imagination. But his hand rests lightly on my waist, and warmth emanates from it.

"Say 'Polly wants a cracker,'" Olivia chirps. Darcy sighs and I roll my eyes. "Yep," Olivia says, holding the phone up to Andrew.

"That's them, all right," Andrew says.

"So what now?" Darcy asks, his voice a whisper in my ear, his breath on my cheek. It smells of cherry coke and vodka. A Vampire Kiss. My foggy brain imagines his mouth lowered to my neck. Nibbling . . .

"What now?" I ask.

"Yeah, Heather," he says, his tone deep. "What now?"

I can't tell what he's asking. Does he want to go home with me, continue our "pass" just a little longer? Or is he asking about the future? Our future. My heart is pounding, and I can't tell if it's with anxiety or arousal. I'm sweating, despite the evening's chill and Darcy's heat. Part of me wants to lean back into him, have that heat envelop me. But the other part? The other part is terrified. The anxiety has settled firmly in my chest. So I do what I've learned to do. I push him away.

"Nothing now, Fitzwilliam," I say. "You go home and when we see each other next, tonight never happened."

His hand on my hip squeezes gently, and then it's gone, along with the warmth of him behind me as he takes a step backwards. A step away.

"If that's what you want," he says quietly, and then louder, "I'm off. Have a good night Olivia. Andrew." He pauses. "Professor Higgins, I'll see you Saturday at the Dean's retirement party if not before." And with that he turns and walks into the night. There's no swagger in his step as I watch him retreat. No, he's just a professor in a pirate's hat. Just like me.

"That was weird," Olivia says. She's also watching him go. "Does he usually call you 'Professor Higgins' outside of school hours?"

"No," I say. "He doesn't."

Andrew comes over and scoops Olivia onto his back, piggyback fashion. Why didn't I have Darcy walk with us? Life's better when you're not the lone pirate. My brain is fuzzy, and all the reasons it wouldn't work seem so easy to brush aside. I could just get another job. Or he could. We could work for the Not-Sexy Librarian. It wouldn't be the end of the world.

But HR is still the minor issue, isn't it? There were reasons I could never be with Darcy. It would mean fitting back into the world I'd chosen to leave behind. Do I really want to do that? No, I don't. I don't want to be stuck somewhere I never fit in with people who look down on me for my father's lack of pedigree or the tattoos on my skin.

But maybe if, after a night of dealing with the snobs and fakeness and barely-masked staring, Darcy would take me home and kiss me like he did . . . Maybe that could make it worth it.

Chapter 44

The blissful in between

I wake up on Friday with a hangover and a smile. I kissed Darcy. That happened. Huh.

I blame the hangover for my fogginess throughout the day. I stop by the Cranky Bean for coffee. Who cares if Benji is there. I kissed Darcy last night. It's nearly one in the afternoon and I still don't regret it.

I've just picked up my drink when a text comes through.

Darcy? No. Stop that, brain. I look down to find a text from my mom.

> Dad and I will be at Dean Mitchell's retirement dinner tomorrow night. Can't wait to see you there!

I didn't know they knew Dean Mitchell, and I can't remember the last time I saw my step-dad, but it doesn't really matter. This is the cost of letting him arrange for my assistant professorship all those years ago,

I suppose. I type a quick reply. At least I'll have Olivia as my plus-one for moral support this time.

My choice to spend the afternoon working in my office has nothing to do with Darcy Delancey. I, unlike the three groupies that poke their heads through my open door to inquire after his whereabouts, am not disappointed by his absence. Not at all.

Chapter 45

Out with the old

Darcy's here with Meredith, the Jane from Monday night. Two Mondays in a row, plus an invite to a work gala. That must mean something.

It shouldn't bother me. I told him there was no future for us. At least, I think that's what I told him. It's possible I just rejected the idea of him coming home and continuing what we'd started outside Fiona's. Our one night pass . . . Either way, I made the right choice. The fact that two nights ago his lips were on mine doesn't give me the right to be upset that he's here with another woman.

But he could have brought Andrew, right? I brought Olivia, after all. I'm not here with some incredible date, just rubbing my desirability in his face. But if he'd brought Andrew, we would inevitably have been together all night. Which, sure, probably wouldn't have been the end of the world. We could have been professional.

"You're staring," Olivia says from beside me.

"Hmm?"

Olivia raises a chin in Darcy's direction.

"It's pure curiosity," I say. "Where does he find them all?"

"He does seem to have a type, doesn't he?"

I've said the same myself, but for some reason hearing it from Olivia's mouth makes it hit home. I am clearly not Darcy's type.

"Heather!" My mother's voice rings out. She's walking towards me, looking lovely in a floor-length maroon dress. I'm wearing the dark teal sheath I wore to the dinner with our mothers. The dress Darcy had to zip up for me. When he called Mima's tattoo beautiful . . . I can't keep myself from glancing his direction. The Jane's hand is on his arm again, and she's smiling.

I return my attention to Mom. Harry, my step-father, has come up behind her in a suit that costs more than my monthly rent. Harry's ten years her senior, but for all of my childhood he seemed frozen in time. "Well-preserved, but unchanged would have been nearer the mark," as Tolkien once said of Bilbo Baggins. Twelve year old me actually asked to see his wedding ring to make sure there was no magical inscription.

But now, five years since I last saw him at the rehearsal dinner, he has aged. He's still handsome, seemingly fit with a well-groomed salt and pepper beard. But beneath it his chin has lost it's firmness and lines have formed around his mouth and eyes.

"Olivia, you know my parents," I say. I know she's never met my step-dad, but saying so would call attention to our estrangement, and I don't want to do that.

"Of course," my mom says, drawing Olivia into a hug. "How are you dear?"

"Very well, Mrs. Randolf." She turns to my father, who shakes her hand with a distracted smile. His eyes have focused in on . . oh. On Darcy.

"I didn't realize the Delancey boy was still teaching here," my father says.

Calling Darcy "the Delancey boy" is a very Harry Randolf II thing to do.

"Yeah, Darcy's still here," I say. "He says you got him his first interview."

"Yes, that I did," Harry says, a slight frown on his face.

"Harry," Mom says, "Olivia and I are headed to the ladies room." Before I can say I'll go along, she adds "Heather will keep you company, and we'll be back straight away."

It's such a mom move, and not one I have the ability to combat. Olivia flashes me an apologetic look as my mother drags her away.

Harry takes two drinks from the tray of a passing waiter and hands one to me. I sip it, trying to ignore the awkward silence that's growing between us. An island of silence in a sea of chit chat. When I can't take it any more I blurt out "I hear Ash is getting married. Mom says his fiancé is lovely."

I take a gulp of my champagne. Harry's eyes dart to where my mom and Olivia have vanished then back to me. "She is very attractive," he says stiffly as he lifts his drink to his lips. "And better than the last one, anyway."

I'd like to believe this means something, indicates some sort of forgiveness or at least a softening towards me, but my stepfather's face remains a pleasant mask. He sips from his champagne, looking around the room rather than at me. As though I'm the least important person there. Then I see the first genuine-looking smile that's crossed his lips since Mom and Olivia left us. Looking up, I see Darcy and his Jane.

"Good evening, Harry," Darcy says, sharing a handshake with my stepfather. "Professor Higgins, always a pleasure," he says to me. Why is my stepdad "Harry" when I've been relegated to formality? He didn't put his tongue in Harry's mouth on Halloween.

"Heather, you've met Meredith," Darcy says. "Meredith, this is Harry Randolf, a long-time family friend."

"I knew this one when he was in diapers," Harry says, not noticing Darcy's subtle wince. "I've been watching your career, Delancey. Always making waves."

None of this is true, not the watching or the waves, but I say nothing.

"It's lovely to meet you, Harry," Meredith says. "Nice to see you again, Professor Higgins."

Her hand is back on Darcy's arm. Is it glued there? Is she making a statement? I hope my smile looks more genuine than it feels.

"Please," I say. "Call me Heather." I lower my brows at Darcy who looks away.

I chat with Meredith, finding out that she's an investment banker who met Darcy through the credit score dating app. It's a good reminder not to judge other women by appearances. This one is not sweet, and I rather like her. Or I would if she weren't here with Darcy.

Harry and Darcy seem to have no trouble carrying on a conversation. I hear bits and pieces as I try to pretend I'm not listening. Darcy asks about Ash as well. Apparently Darcy has been invited to the ceremony. He tells Harry he hasn't decided yet if he'll be attending, eyes darting to me and then away. Am I imagining it, or did they soften for just a moment?

I feel an arm slip into mine and find Olivia beside me. I don't know whether she's heard or just read my face, but I'm grateful that she's here.

At this point a voice from the podium calls us all to our seats as dinner service is about to begin. Darcy will have no need to collect me from the nose-bleed section, as he did at the *Jane, Reimagined* awards. No, I find myself seated at one of the front tables along with my parents and Olivia and several other faculty members. I notice that Tweed, the Not-sexy Librarian and Darcy are seated in similar positions. I would have thought they'd put us all together, as our presentation is the final one of the night, the one meant to reassure everyone present that the future of the Liberal Arts College at Springvale is secure. But no, we are clearly meant to showcase our schmoozing abilities with the bigwigs present, my step-father included. Tonight must be the final piece of the interview process. After all, it's Dean Mitchell's farewell. The college will want a new person at the head as soon as possible.

I glance at the Dean, seated at a table nearby. What must that be like? His wife is beside him, all smiles, and I feel bad for believing the gossip Olivia told me. Darcy, who knew him well, hadn't believed it. He believed the best about people, even those who, like me, so often didn't deserve it. I can't keep myself from glancing his way, and when I do I find his gaze on me. He smiles just a little and lifts his glass. I lift mine in return. Then Meredith says something and Darcy turns his attention to her.

They would make a beautiful couple. She's the first of the Janes I could see him with. Sure, we didn't talk long, but she's smart. Clever and maybe even a touch snarky. Maybe not a Jane after all.

She reminds me of- oh crap. Of me.

What have I done?

Chapter 46

And the winner is . . .

As the evening continues, I wonder if everyone else had a different experience with Dean Mitchell than I did. I want to give this new strategy of Darcy's, this "assume the best" attitude, a try. Unfortunately I don't know how to reconcile it with a Dean who, despite seeing me every two weeks for the past five years, still forgets my name on a regular basis.

As I hear story after story, I begin to wonder if I'm just that underwhelming. That peripheral.

Sitting with my stepfather isn't helping. Now that Mom has returned as a buffer, all obligation to talk to me has vanished. Still, surrounded by my mom on one side and Olivia on the other, I'm handling the night well enough. When the final stories have been told and awards for service presented, Darcy, Tweed, Pfisten and I are called to the stage.

I take my place beside Darcy, doing my best not to squirm as the Provost begins a speech about the admirable young leaders who will take the University into the next era with their passion and ingenuity. I can't help but wonder how this speech is given in the science departments. Are they commended for leading with data-driven matrixes and, I don't know, some other science-oriented word?

Darcy steps forward to introduce our presentation then cues the sound techs to roll film. It's impressive, really, how we managed to cobble our disparate views of how this college should be run into one buzz-word heavy, substance-light six minute propaganda extravaganza. When it ends Professor Pfisten makes our closing remarks, and the Provost regains the podium. I expect a last call for polite applause and to be allowed to take my seat, but that isn't what happens.

Instead the Provost waits until he has everyone's attention and begins speaking again.

"As you all know, Dean Mitchell has captained this department well for the past eight years, and it is with heavy, yet joyful, hearts that we send him forth into his next voyage. Each of the candidates before you is equipped to masterfully navigate the upcoming seas of . . ."

This is where I lose track of what the Provost is saying. When did he turn into a navy recruiter? Somehow my mind has wandered to Darcy in his pirate's hat, right before . . . Wait. Everyone is clapping again. A glance to my right shows Pfisten's tight, forced smile. Is her forehead twitching? A glance at the audience shows Olivia, her eyes twice their normal size. Beside her my mother beams. Harry looks smug.

"Damn it!" Tweed says, throwing the program he was holding on the floor. He stomps off the stage and out the side door. In the audience a stout woman in a loud floral dress who I assume must be his poor, unsatisfied wife, gathers her things and hurries after him.

Suddenly I'm back at Ash's rehearsal dinner . . . What is going on? I've obviously missed something important.

"You should probably shake hands with the Provost," Darcy says from my elbow. "Thank him and 'take the helm,' so to speak."

"You've got to be kidding me," I say. "They didn't."

"They did."

Murmuring has started in the audience, and I realize that if I don't do something soon my first act as Dean will be to humiliate myself in front of the entirety of the department and its largest donors.

"Dean Higgins," the Provost says, "I see I've left you speechless. Surely this can't be that much of a surprise. Please, come over and say a few words."

"Of course," I say. I walk to the Provost, shake his hand, say some sort of BS to the crowd. It must be the right thing, because the polite applause continues. Apparently my words have righted the ship.

Chapter 47

The Morning After

I wake up to sun streaming through my windows. Fumbling for my phone on the nightstand, I read 9:33. How in the world did I sleep this long? I barely even drank.

Sinking back into my pillow, I relive the schmooze-fest that occurred after the Provost's announcement. I must have accepted congratulations from everyone in the room. Well, with the exception of Professor Pfisten who, to her credit, slipped out rather than putting on a show like Tweed.

Darcy's congratulations, given both on the stage and afterwards with Meredith on his arm, seemed genuine. My promotion didn't seem to put a damper on his evening, which bothered me for two reasons, only one of which I'm willing to acknowledge.

This job should have been his. He's clearly the better candidate. Heck, he actually cares if the students are learning something.

I did catch him with a scowl on his face once, when he was talking with ex-Dean Mitchell. I only noticed because it was an expression formerly absent from my Darcy catalogue. He and Meredith must have left soon after, because I didn't see him again.

Meredith . . . he really brought Meredith to the dinner after Halloween? Maybe he invited her before the kiss. Or maybe he took me at my word when I said "this night never happened."

I force thoughts of Darcy Delancey from my mind.

Harry was happy, anyway. When my mother complained of a headache soon after the announcement and Olivia offered to drive her home, Harry stayed by my side. He shook hands and exchanged small talk with all of the well-wishers who sought me out. It felt good to have him there and so obviously proud of me. Good enough that I understand why Ash idolizes him. Good enough that I start thinking things could be different now.

Was the approval conditional? Sure. But it still felt like waking up in Ithilien and finding everything right with the world. (You know, how at the end of the Lord of the Rings trilogy . . . wait, that's a spoiler. If you haven't read it, just read the book already. And for now, know that it felt too good to be true.)

I crawl from my bed and make my way to the kitchen. Olivia has left a note on the counter letting me know that she's going furniture shopping with Andrew after church and not to expect her home before late afternoon. She ended it with "Congratulations, Dean!" and a smiley.

That's Olivia. Trying to put a positive spin on something she knows might actually be a problem. I bet it killed her to be gone today, but it's good for me. I need this time to process and recharge.

I push the required buttons on the Keurig and unwrap a granola bar while I wait.

My mind goes back to the question that's been circling since that insane announcement last night.

Who in the world was irresponsible enough to make me Dean?

I shouldn't be Dean of a preschool, let alone a college. And while I understand the "whos" involved, I must be missing something with the "why." My best theory is that there's been a ridiculous mistake and on Monday morning I'll find an email with a brief apology and a retraction of the offer.

Harry will be disappointed, but that's normal.

I'm staring into my coffee cup and contemplating these deep thoughts when there's a knock on the door. A glance at my phone shows it's almost ten now. Late enough that someone's trying to sell me windows, or maybe their religion.

When I open the door, I find Darcy. My heart gives a little flip and I tell it to behave.

But, he's here . . .

"Heather," Darcy says, "I need to talk with you. May I come in?"

Does he want to figure out a way to be together, even with me as Dean? But I don't want to be Dean, and I haven't had time to think this all through yet. Still . . .

I've been hesitating too long.

"Sorry. Yes, of course. Come in."

I usher Darcy in and close the door behind him.

"Would you like a coffee?" I ask. "Or tea? We have something herbal that Olivia swears by."

"Water would be good," Darcy says. He seems nervous. Or agitated, maybe?

I hand him his glass of water and motion towards the table. Darcy takes a seat, and I take the one beside him, rather than across. And

211

then there's silence, last night's promotion sitting squarely on the table between us. Should I address it? Before I can, Darcy begins.

"Last night was a surprise," he says. "I didn't realize the decision had been made."

"I didn't either," I say. "Not until the Provost's announcement. Or a touch after."

I intend it to lighten the mood, but Darcy's gaze is serious. Why is he looking at me so intently? Does he want to know how I'm feeling about the new position? About it's ramifications for us?

Not that there is an "us." But does he want there to be?

"Heather," Darcy continues, looking at his hands, which are fidgeting with a napkin from the table, and then back at my face. "This is hard to say, but I think the direct approach is best."

Oh, God. He does want us to be together. My heart has sped up, and I really hope I'm not sweating. I haven't put on deodorant this morning. I'm leaning towards him, not by choice, but because my body, at least, is ready to say "yes." We can figure out the details of how it will all work later. I look away from his lips, which I've apparently been staring at, and back to his eyes. He's waiting on me to say something. To give him permission to continue. I can do better than words.

I lean forward and bring my mouth to his. His hesitation lasts only a moment, and then he's kissing me back. It's not like Halloween, which was only a few nights ago, but seems like forever. No, it's hungrier. Maybe a little desperate. I understand how he feels. This is what I've wanted. Heck, it was practically fated from birth, and I don't know why it's taken me so long to quit fighting it.

But then his hands are on my shoulders, and instead of pulling me closer he's gently putting me away from him. Not far, but far enough.

"We need to talk first," he says.

I nod, looking longingly at those lips. It's so Darcy. First we need to figure out the logistics, the rules, how to do it right. And then we can go back to the kissing.

"I'm sorry," he says, "but this is important."

"I know," I say. "And I'm sure there's a way we can navigate it. I mean, really, I don't even know if I want the Dean position. But if it's not me, it will be you, and then we'd still need to figure this out."

Darcy looks confused. Normally I love that expression, but right now it sends a shot of anxiety through me.

"You know, with HR and all?" I say.

"Ah. Yes, that. We'll need to talk through that as well, but that's not why I came," Darcy says. He rushes on. "Dean Mitchell told me something last night, and I think you would want to know."

I remember Darcy's scowl, the one I hadn't seen before, and dread displaces the butterflies in my stomach.

"What is it?" I ask.

"Your stepfather just made a very, very large donation to the Liberal Arts College."

For a moment time stops. There it is. The answer I'd been looking for. But now I don't think I want it.

"I didn't know," I say.

Darcy nods. "I figured that."

Oh my God. I'm such an idiot. I knew there had to be a reason they'd make me Dean. I'm glad Darcy didn't assume I was part of this, but it's still humiliating.

"Does everyone know?" I ask. If Dean Mitchell told Darcy, he probably told other people too.

"I don't know," Darcy says, those beautiful lips of his turning down. "But it's public record. I checked before I came over, in case Mitchell was wrong."

"So if everyone doesn't know, they will," I say.

Darcy's back to fiddling with the napkin. Fiddling with . . . Oh my God.

"That's what you came to tell me. You weren't here to figure out how we could navigate a relationship with the HR rules and all of that at all. You were here to tell me my stepfather bought my promotion. And then I stuck my tongue down your throat."

"Heather," Darcy begins, but I stop him.

"Did you kiss Meredith last night?" I ask.

He looks away then back at me, and I know he did. He starts to reply but I cut him off again.

"It's none of my business," I say. "I shouldn't have asked."

Somehow the humiliation keeps compounding, and then it does what it always does. It turns to anger. At my stepfather, and how he purchased a reason to be proud of me. He was accepting his own congratulations last night.

And at Darcy who told me about it, even though this isn't his fault. But he kissed me and then Meredith and then me again, all in less than four days time. I don't care if there was a pass involved or that I was the instigator both times. The rational part of my brain has officially left the kitchen.

"You know what," I say, "You should go."

"Heather, there's no reason for me to leave. We need to talk through this."

I know if I let him stay I'll say something I regret, so instead I say something I regret.

"There's no 'we,' Fitzwilliam," I say. "*I* need to think through this. I'll see you at the office."

His brows lower. That beautiful mouth opens, closes, opens again, and ends in a frown. And part of me wants him to stay and fight me. To quit being the gentleman and make me hear him out.

But he doesn't. He nods once, stands and walks to the door.

I think he must look back, but I don't look up at him, just lean my head in my hands and listen for the door to snick closed. He's too polite even to slam it like I deserve.

The tattoo I don't get

I know better now, after the Queen's crown and the lotus. And maybe the larkspur. Sometimes it takes me a while to learn.

But I know now not to get a tattoo when I'm upset.

I want one. Maybe a bleeding and ravaged heart wrapped in barbed wire to remind me that letting someone too close is always, always painful. Maybe a big scarlet "N" for Nepotism placed boldly for everyone to see. I've been part of the faculty rumor mill. There's only one way this will go. It's probably some sort of cosmic retribution that Dean Mitchell was the one who told Darcy. Live by the sword, die by the sword, and all that. Unfortunately, I'm too angry and confused to appreciate it.

Darcy.

I kicked him out, and not in a nice way. If there is a nice way to reject someone for the tenth time. Twentieth?

He really is a fool for coming back. He's better off with Meredith. She seems way more emotionally stable than I am. He can have Meredith and I can be alone.

Always alone.

I text Olivia and tell her not to let me get a tattoo for at least a week, and then I close my curtains on the bright morning sunshine and curl up in bed to wait for sleep to come.

Chapter 48

Nepotism much?

I wake up mid-afternoon and text my mom.

> **Did you know?**

>> Know what?

> **That Harry was making a large donation to the college.**

>> . . .

The dots stay there for a long time and finally my phone rings. I send it to voicemail. Mom texts again.

>> Heather, pick up your phone.

> **Sorry. I can't.**

It's a lie, but not really. I don't trust myself to talk to her right now.

>> Why not?

Instead of answering I double down.

Did you know?

Yes, but it's not a big deal. You would have gotten the promotion anyway.

I guess we'll never know, will we. And btw, now my authority with the department is entirely undermined. There will always be people who think I bought this job.

That's not true, Heather. You'll be a wonderful Dean. In a year, no one will even remember the donation.

There's no sense in arguing with her. If I do, I'll just look ungrateful; I'm sure a deanship isn't cheap.

The crazy thing in all of this is that I have no desire to be dean. Zero. Cero. Nada. Zilch. Every culture and subculture on Earth has a way to say none, and I want to be dean that much in each and every language.

Should I decline it? I could decline the position and all of this would go away. I didn't ask Harry to do this, so it's not my fault if his money is wasted.

I make the mistake of opening my email while pondering my options. Sandwiched between several congratulations notes is yet another rejection letter from an agent. Because why wouldn't there be? Obviously no one, with the exception of Darcy and a couple of my online friends, likes my take on fantasy. Darcy, who I rejected and threw out of my house this morning.

What am I doing?

Maybe I should just suck it up and be Dean. It would make my parents proud, and surely all of my creative energy and aspirations would be crushed beneath the weight of schmoozing and responsibility. Then I wouldn't have to worry about rejection letters.

I can't do it.

I won't.

I'm going to email the Provost and decline the offer. But first I need to tell Harry in person.

Chapter 49

The best surprise

I'm on the way to the luxury condo Mom and Harry moved into once Ash was in college when the text comes through. I glance at my phone, expecting Olivia or my Mom. Maybe even Darcy, who's a kind enough human that he might text to make sure I'm ok, even after I'm awful to him.

Instead the screen is lit up with a picture of Ash at eight years old wearing that KC Chiefs jersey that never left his body. My baby brother, who has blocked all conversation since the night I ruined his rehearsal dinner, has texted me.

I pull into a strip mall and park in an empty spot, then pick up my phone with shaking hands. The text really is from Ash.

> **Hi Sis. Long time no talk. Congratulations on making dean.**

I blink down at the screen. It's so casual, like he hasn't blocked me from his life for years. Is he serious? Does he know I've cried more tears over him than over everything else ever combined?

I read the text again before replying. I can't mess this up. If he blocks me again, I don't think my heart could take it. Especially not right now. I erase and rewrite my text several times before forcing myself to send.

> Ash! It's good to hear from you. Thank you. And congratulations to you as well.

I wait, hoping for dots, but there are no dots. Do I write him again? Ask a question so he has to reply? Before I can decide, another message comes through.

> We should talk. And my fiancé wants to meet you. We'll be in KC later this week for a bridal shower Mom's throwing. Do you want to get coffee?

Mom hasn't mentioned a shower, but she wouldn't. I wouldn't have been invited, and she wouldn't have rubbed that in.

> I would love to. When? Where?

I know I sound too eager, but I've already hit send. Ash is really texting me. He wouldn't be doing this if he weren't willing to forgive me, would he? Oh, God, please.

> We're staying at the Intercontinental. Can you meet in their lobby Thursday morning at 9?

> I'll see you there.

He clicks my message with a thumbs up, and then there's nothing. I sit in my car and cry, then I turn on the car and drive back home. I can't confront Harry. Harry senior. Not today. I can't rock this boat. Not when there's a chance of having Ash back in my life.

Chapter 50

A knight in shining armor

When I get home I find Olivia and Andrew in the kitchen with a "congratulations" cake. Chocolate, because Olivia loves me so very much.

"Where were you?" Olivia asks. I fill them in on my morning visit from Darcy, the nepotism and the text from Ash. How I can't call Harry out if Ash might finally be willing to forgive me.

Olivia is unconvinced, but supportive as usual.

Actually, not quite as usual. Olivia's slice of cake is nearly untouched, and her eyes are pinched.

"What's going on?" I ask.

"Headache," Olivia says. A look passes between her and Andrew that I can't decipher, then Olivia excuses herself to her room. Andrew follows with water and ibuprofen. When he returns I'm still sitting at the table. I've taken the frosting off of Olivia's slice and pushed it to one side of the plate so I can get at the cake itself, which I'm savoring, one delicious forkful at a time.

"You don't deserve her," Andrew says.

"Excuse me?" I look up, surprised.

"You don't deserve Olivia." Andrew says slowly, like he's talking to a child.

I'm more confused than angry. "She's the best person on the planet," I say. "No one deserves her. But why are you telling me this?"

"Do you even know her dad's sick?"

"What?"

I must have said that loudly, because Andrew shushes me with a nod towards the hallway where my amazing best friend is in bed with a headache. He practically spits out his next words, all while keeping his voice at a whisper level.

"Olivia's dad was diagnosed with colon cancer. She found out Saturday, but she didn't want to bring it into your 'big night.' She's been stressed out all day about needing to get home, but she doesn't want to flake on your birthday plans and leave you all alone. You've been too self-absorbed to notice."

I'm speechless. And I always have words. Words are my sword and shield, but Andrew has disarmed me.

"And while I'm at it, this poor little rich girl thing is getting old. We're all born somewhere and maybe you fit in, maybe you don't. You get over it, you don't let it define you."

I've never seen Andrew like this. Where is the eager to please, take-out offering man who's been in my house the last few weeks?

"OK, hold up," I say. "Olivia's dad is sick?"

"Yeah," Andrew says. "And you'd know that if you'd quit seeing her as your sidekick and see her for the amazing woman she is."

225

Okay, that's a step too far and completely unwarranted. It is unwarranted, isn't it?

"I know she's amazing," I say. "I'd have kicked you out if you weren't saying all this crap in her defense. But now, I think you'd better go. Because we still need to know each other and I need to process so I don't say something we'll all wish I hadn't."

But apparently once Andrew gets started he's hard to shut down, because he continues like I haven't said a word.

"And the way you treat Darcy . . . I have no idea why he keeps coming back for more."

"Hold on," I say. My voice must have gotten loud because Andrew's eyes dart back towards the bedrooms and they're shooting fire when they look my way again. I continue in a hissed whisper. "I get what you said about Olivia, but I haven't done anything to Darcy."

"Oh, no. Of course not. You haven't made out with him and then rejected him twice already this week."

"He told you that?" I ask.

"Of course not," Andrew says. "You know the man. But I have eyes. It's not like the two of you were subtle on Halloween, and Olivia and I came back to grab her glasses after church and almost walked in on your little 'conversation,' only to see Darcy leave like a kicked dog a few minutes later."

"You have no idea what was going on there," I say.

"Of course not. How could I possibly understand trying to work with a woman who simultaneously drives me insane and feels as necessary as breathing?" Andrew asks. "Darcy's better off with Meredith anyway."

And with that parting thrust, he's gone. Out the front door, closing it gently for Olivia's sake, and leaving me frothing in his wake.

Chapter 51

Main characters

Olivia stays in her room the rest of Sunday night. I check on her a couple times, bring new water and ibuprofen, but she sleeps through it. Which is a good thing when a migraine hits. Olivia doesn't get migraines often, usually only when unusual amounts of stress and her period coincide, but when she does, they're bad.

She's still asleep when I leave for my first class the next morning. I put out her favorite tea and fill the kettle on the stove with water, as though saving her fifteen seconds will make up for being the crappiest friend on the planet. What Andrew said has really gotten into my head, and I vacillate between being pissed at him and pissed at myself. It's mostly at myself, though.

I leave her a note, something positive and Olivia-esq, and ask her to text me to let me know how she's feeling once she wakes up. The text comes through while I'm lecturing, and I reply as soon as class is over. Olivia is feeling better, and yes, she'd love a girls night tonight.

I reply that I'll pick up dinner.

The day is packed with congratulations from colleagues and emails from the HR department. Olivia and I took Thursday and Friday off to celebrate our birthdays, so the BIG MEETING with the provost, HR and who knows who else will be Monday, one week from today.

If it weren't for Ash, this nightmare would already be over. I tell myself that I can handle being Dean for a semester, maybe a year, if it will keep me in my brother's good graces. I'm not sure it's true, and slightly resentful that it took this promotion to make Ash finally reach out, but I stuff that down. Those feelings won't get me my brother back.

It feels weird not to be meeting with Darcy and Pfisten tonight. I refuse to be nostalgic for Tweed, but still . . .

Olivia knows something is up the moment I walk through the door with gyros and baklava.

Her eyebrows scrunch down, and her head tilts sideways.

"Am I dying?" Olivia asks.

"No," I say. "But Andrew told me your dad is sick. And I'm sorry I didn't realize something was wrong. I should have, if I wasn't so wrapped up in my own drama."

Olivia's shoulders slump. "I'm sorry I have to add this to your load right now," she says, and my heart breaks just a little bit more.

"Olivia, you're my best friend. It doesn't need to be you carrying me all the time. Tell me about what's going on. What do you need to do?"

So she does. It turns out her parents have known there was a problem for several months, but kept it from her until they were more certain what was going on.

"So do you want a ride to the airport?" I ask.

"Andrew really has been chatty, hasn't he?" Olivia says.

"He was just looking out for you." As I say it I realize it's true, and regret again that I wasn't the one looking out for Olivia.

"Then, yeah, you can drive me," she says. "I'll tell Andrew he's in charge of pickup." Olivia is chewing on her lip and looking guilty. "What will you do on your birthday?" she asks. "I'm ruining all our plans."

"Hopefully things will go well with Ash and I'll be at Zoe's bridal shower on my birthday," I say. Oh, please, let it be so.

Olivia frowns, just a quick dip of the corner of her mouth, but I see it.

"What?" I ask.

"Nothing."

"Tell me."

"Fine. I'm still mad that your mom planned Zoe's shower on your thirtieth birthday," she says.

"It's not her fault," I say. "I told her I was busy." I realize my mistake when Olivia's face falls. I hurry on. "Plus, Ash wouldn't have texted if he didn't want to see me. I'm sure I'll get to go and that will be the best birthday gift ever."

Olivia doesn't look convinced, but she forces a smile.

Chapter 52

Fiancé, Hotel Lobby, Deception (take 2)

I'm there early. Not so early that it's stalkerish or anything, but early.

The morning was glorious, and we're into that time of November where you treat every beautiful day like the last, so I decided to walk. Maps told me it would take twenty minutes, but there was no way I was showing up late and risking missing him. So here I am, coffee cup in hand, waiting in a plush seat that's pointed towards the elevators as I scan every face for my brother.

They didn't have pistachio syrup, but I'm choosing not to see this as a sign. The mocha I'm drinking is more than adequate. For a mocha, anyway.

"Heather?" I look up at a slim brunette with warm brown eyes and a tentative smile. It's Zoe, Ash's fiancé. She looks just like her pics on the socials, maybe even prettier.

Before I can stand, she sits down in the seat beside me. I glance all around, but Ash is nowhere to be seen. Zoe's smile dims. "It's just me for now," she says. "I'm Zoe."

"It's really nice to meet you," I say. And it is.

This woman is Ash's future. She's wearing yoga pants and a long soccer club sweatshirt. In this lobby filled with brand names and business suits, she's a hobbit among elves. Despite her casual clothing, the gentleness radiating off her makes her the most beautiful woman in the room.

"Do you want me to grab you a coffee?" I ask.

"Nah, I'm good," Zoe says. "I've wanted to meet you for a long time."

"Same here," I say.

"Your brother misses you," Zoe says. Apparently we're diving right in. "Did you know he got a tattoo? It's not on his Insta."

"He did?"

"Yeah. On his calf. It matches yours."

"Harold?" I ask, tears I can't keep back springing to my eyes.

Zoe nods. "We'd been dating for six months before he told me about it."

She's everything I hoped she'd be, from her generic tennis shoes to her rich laugh. Time is passing and still Ash isn't here. Fifteen minutes, then half an hour goes by. Zoe tells me how they met. I finish my adequate mocha. Should I ask when Ash will join us?

And then he's there. Standing by a pillar scanning the room. His eyes light up when he sees Zoe, and then his gaze falls on me. Hurt flickers across his face, and then there's nothing, the light that was there snuffed out.

Chapter 53

The reckoning

He didn't know I'd be here. I should have guessed it when Zoe was the one who met me, not Ash. No, not Ash ushering her forward, so excited, like he had the first time with Kitty, before it all went wrong.

You know that pain you get sometimes, in the back of your jaw, when you're about to cry?

Zoe's hand on my arm recenters me. I don't remember looking down, but I look up at her now. Her brown eyes, still warm, do little to reassure me. "I believe he's a good man, Heather. He'll forgive you."

And with that she gets up and walks to my brother. I can't hear what she says, but she reaches up on tiptoes and kisses his cheek. She squeezes his arm, just like she did mine. And then, with one last wave and tense smile my way, she's gone.

For a moment I think Ash is going to leave. Turn and follow her. But he doesn't. Instead, he walks slowly my way. Should I stand? He's looming over me before I can decide, and then he's taken the chair Zoe left vacant.

He still isn't looking at me. Instead he stares at his hands, clenched together between legs that are casually splayed. The clenching is what's real. Despite his practiced calm, Ash's hands have always given him away. I would speak, but I don't know what to say. Finally, I have to break the silence.

"I'm sorry," I say. It's what I've wanted to tell him for so long.

"Sorry for what, Heather?" he asks. And I know it's a test. One I don't want to fail.

"I'm sorry I handled it so badly. Sorry I didn't find a way to tell you sooner."

"Sorry you humiliated me in front of everyone important to me?" Ash says.

"Yes," I say, dread settling in my gut. "I'm sorry for that."

"Why, Heather?" his voice is barely leashed fury scraping through clenched teeth. "Why did you do it that way? How long did you know?"

Oh, he's going to hate me. Even more than he did already.

"Do you remember when Kitty took that trip home to Georgia, right before you got engaged?" I ask.

Ash's nod is short, a quick bob of acknowledgement.

"She wasn't in Georgia. I saw her with Ant at a hotel in Phoenix."

Ash swears under his breath. I stammer on.

"I tried to call you, but it went to voicemail and that's not something you leave in a message. And then when you came home at Easter, you were engaged and wanting a quick wedding. Mima died and there were the graduations and everything fell apart. I watched them, and convinced myself maybe it was just that one time or I'd misunderstood somehow. I was a coward. But that night I knew, and I couldn't let you do it. I couldn't let you ruin your life."

"You couldn't let me ruin my life?" Ash asks, incredulous. "So what, you decided to do it for me?"

I can't speak, can't reply, because I can't breathe. It's like when I fell from the neighbor's tree onto my back and lay there gasping for I don't know how long, afraid I'd never be able to draw a breath again.

Ash looks up at my silence and the pain in his eyes . . . I close my eyes to escape it, but there is no escaping. I run my fingers along my neck, think of my Dad's eagle tattooed there. Of his death. I've always known I wouldn't have Ash had he survived, and for a long time it was a comfort, but there is no comfort now. No comfort anywhere.

"I've got to go, Heather," Ash says, rising. "Don't go behind my back to Zoe like this again. She's the best thing that's ever happened to me, and I don't want you near her."

I can't speak. Can't get the words out to tell him she reached out to me. That I thought it was him I was meeting with.

I whisper "I'm sorry" towards his retreating form, but it's too low for him to hear it.

Chapter 54

Vodka and tissues

I wake up to banging and a female voice calling my name.

I'm on the couch, neck crooked at an awkward angle against the armrest. I rub at the sand in my eyes and squint against the morning light. The room wobbles as I make it to sitting and place both feet on the floor. The pounding continues, resonating through my skull. I try to call out that I'm coming, anything to make it stop, but my mouth is dry enough that I cough at the air going down my throat. Somehow I manage to stumble to the front door and pull it open.

"Heather? Oh, thank God."

My mother looks simultaneously relieved and appalled. Her hands flutter up and around me, pulling me into a hug. "Oh, my sweet girl," she breathes into my hair. "I'm so glad you're ok."

Over her shoulder my step-father surveys the cobwebs in the rafters of my porch.

Mom pulls back from the hug and looks into my face, her mouth turning down as she realizes "ok" might be a stretch.

I wander towards the kitchen in search of water and ibuprofen, leaving the front door open behind me. Leaning back against the counter, I swallow both down. I rub my hands across my eyes and over my face, then stretch my shoulders.

"Why wouldn't I be ok, Mom," I ask, wondering which of the many reasons has her showing up at my house at the crack of dawn.

"We got the email from the provost, and then you wouldn't answer your phone," she says. "I was afraid you'd done something drastic."

Drastic? Like . . . wow. Just, wow. I didn't see that coming.

"Why did you think that, Mom?" I ask. I walk back towards the living room. My parents still linger near the doorway. I follow Harry's gaze to the throw pillows strewn on the ground and the nearly-empty bottle of vodka sitting on the coffee table. There's not even a glass nearby.

"People sever ties before they do that sort of thing," Mom says. "And tomorrow is your thirtieth birthday. Lots of creative types go at 29, you know."

I didn't know. I'm not sure I understand what she's implying even now. I also have no idea how I got home from Ash's hotel, although I assume I walked, or what I did the rest of the day. Hell, I'm not even sure when I bought that bottle of vodka.

Did she say they got an email from the provost?

"What do you mean you got an email from the provost?" I ask.

My mother's eyes dart to Harry and back to me.

Before she can speak, Harry takes over. "I received an email from the provost informing me that you had declined the role of Dean. Imagine his surprise, after you'd done so well in the interview process and we'd come to such a friendly agreement regarding terms."

I declined the role of Dean? Now that he says it, I do remember typing an email to that affect . . . Wait.

"Did you just say a friendly agreement regarding terms?" I ask. "Are you admitting you bought me that position?"

"Of course not," Harry says. "Don't be absurd."

"What does that mean, then?" I ask. I was squinting already, what with the vodka and the stupid sunshine coming through the windows (it hurts us, precious), but now my eyes must be slits. My inner dragon would be proud.

"I mean that you were a perfectly qualified applicant in a race against other perfectly qualified applicants, and on occasion it doesn't hurt to show your loyalty to an institution in a tangible way," Harry says.

"You've got to be kidding," I growl. "Did it ever occur to you that I might want to be good enough on my own merit? Or maybe that I didn't even want the job?"

From the look on Harry's face, it had not.

"Heather," says my mom, ever the peace-maker. "What's really going on? I know you haven't been happy, especially since you and Darcy broke up, but this seems a bit extreme."

How did my mother know about Darcy? Oh, she means that night at dinner. My eyes dart to Harry and back to my mom. She gives him a look, and he excuses himself to the restroom.

Mom replaces the throw pillows and sits on the couch. She pats the cushion beside her and I collapse into it.

"What's really going on?" Mom asks again.

So I tell her about Ash. I see the pain that mars her face before she covers it with forced optimism and platitudes about time. True to form, I hadn't thought about how hard it must be for my mom to bear the rift between her children. I'd just thought about myself. And Ash. I thought about Ash.

By the time Harry returns I resemble a human again, albeit a ragged one. Mom has wrung the last of the tears from my body and swept the soggy tissues into the trash can. She's extracted a promise that I'll drink water and eat something healthy, although she's not naive enough to clarify what exactly "healthy" means in this context.

She's done what she always does. She's picked me up so I can soldier on. And me? I've let her, lying when necessary, pretending I believe Ash will ever forgive me. Because for once I'm thinking about what others need, and my mother needs that to be true.

As she follows Harry to the door, Mom pulls a small bag from her purse and places it on the table.

"For your birthday tomorrow," she says with one last forced smile.

Chapter 55

Happy Birthday to Me

I missed Kansas City when I was away for undergrad. Los Angeles never gave the gift my city gives on my thirtieth birthday. No, in LA when life is crumbling the city gives you sunshine. Even the infrequent rain was refreshing, a renewal that washed the smog off the trees and set up the desert foliage for another month without water. You could enjoy it because you knew it wouldn't last forever, as ephemeral as life itself.

But KC is my spirit city. It can be counted on to know my mood. On my thirtieth birthday, the sun doesn't rise.

I mean, fine. It rises. Somewhere far away the earth has tilted and people bask in its light. But here, in my city, grey sleet pounds the muddy earth, stripping the reds and oranges and yellows from the trees. This morning, my city gets me.

I lay in bed for hours staring through my parted curtains at the lone tree along our fence-line. Its crisp, brown leaves fall, one after another. Eventually my full bladder forces me from bed. I shamble from the bathroom to the kitchen, consider ordering in good coffee, and finally settling on tea.

While I wait on the tea kettle to whistle, I notice my mom's gift still on the table.

Pulling the card from the bag, I read the sappy outer words about watching a daughter grow. On the inside, Mom has written "I want you to know that I do believe in your dreams, and I'm very proud of you Heather."

Well, that's nice. I sniffle a couple of times, not exactly sure what to do with the emotions I'm having.

Then I pull the small box wrapped in silver paper from the bag. I peel it back carefully to find a fountain pen inside.

Fancy. Classy. Expensive.

I grab the notepad from the fridge to try it out.

Heather Higgins is not a loser, I write in my best cursive, then laugh down at the paper. Who am I kidding?

Thirty is the new twenty.

Ha.

Darcy Delancey is a coward.

Where did that come from? I mean, yeah, he gives up pretty easily. But I've given him no reason not to.

Heather Higgins is a coward.

Heather Higgins is a coward. And there's the truth of it.

The kettle shrieks and I startle.

And you know what? I've had enough of this. Enough of the pity and oblivion. Enough of the vodka and its resulting damage to my no longer young cranium, not to mention my liver.

If I have to feel miserable, I'm going to use it.

Taking my pen and hot tea with me, I walk back to my bedroom and sit down at the computer.

I type. And it's the best thing I've written in a long time. Hopefully Olivia's theory of character kharma is off the rails because if not my next decade is screwed.

My poor heroine is trapped. Her cell, an expansive cavern when the tide is out, shrinks to a tiny, underground island when the tide comes in. She knows how she got here, and there's no comfort in it. She's here because of choices she made. Knowingly. Willingly. She has trapped herself in the dark, and though she explores every nook of it with her cut and bruised fingers, there is no escape.

No way she can free herself.

And that's when it turns. When she realizes that there's nothing else she can do.

When I realize the same thing.

Ash will forgive me, or he won't. And I can't let his choices determine my future.

An agent will love my writing, or she won't. That doesn't mean I shouldn't write what I love.

I can't control Ash or Harry or my mother or Olivia.

Or Darcy.

Oh, I can't even think about the mess I've made with Darcy right now.

But I can control me. I take a deep breath and keep writing. I write for hours, long enough to free my heroine and myself.

The rain still falls in sheets as I finish, but that's ok.

I'm re-reading what I've written when there's a ping on my phone. I didn't order food, but my app tells me something has been delivered. Rising I open the front door to find a box of donuts with a note.

"Thought you might forget our birthday tradition. Eat these and think of me. Be home soon."

I call Olivia, but it goes to voicemail where I leave the peppiest thank you I can muster. Then I make myself a cup of coffee and choose a glorious creme filled, chocolate frosted middle finger to my waistline from the box. It's too sweet, even paired with my bitter brew, but I relish every bite.

I take my donut and coffee to the couch with me. This isn't where I thought I'd be at thirty, but that's ok. How could twenty-something me, all bright and shiny and innocent, have guessed that I'd turn thirty alone with my only friend across the country? That I'd have declined a huge promotion that would have made my life miserable? Actually, twenty year old me should be proud of that. Thirty year old me is.

The ridiculous part is that I let myself get sucked into the running for a job I never wanted because I didn't want to back down to Darcy, a man who never should have been my nemesis, but was at the wrong place at the wrong time and suffered my wrath because of it.

Darcy who's probably about to be my new boss, and who will do a much better job in the role than I ever would have. Dad won't even have to ask for a refund. I'm betting if he'd remembered Darcy was still working at the college he'd have put his money on Darcy anyway. Darcy with those blue eyes that crinkle in the corner when he smiles. The man who is universally liked because he genuinely likes everyone, even his cave-dwelling linguistics-professor colleague.

Darcy who might be out with Meredith right now. And he should be. She's not a Jane, despite all appearances. She'll be good for him.

The fact that there's no man in my life at thirty shouldn't matter, and it wouldn't if it weren't for that stupid Jane Austen writing contest. But now that I've opened that door, it's hard to push all these longings back inside.

When I tattooed that dragonfly I had no idea. No idea how long this other dream would be on hold. Thirty was a lifetime away.

I can feel the peace and epiphany that came from writing leaching from my soul, and decide to hop online with my fantasy forum before I can slide any further. First, though, a quick scan of my email.

Wait. What?

I blink and read twice, pinch myself, close out of my email and reopen it. It's still there.

From: Carmen@CarmenAlexander.com
To: HeatherHigginsAuthor@gmail.com
Ms. Higgins,
*Your manuscript for **The Winter Mist** is exactly what I've been looking for. Are you available for a chat at my offices on Monday?*
Sincerely,
Carmen Alexander

How is that possible?

I pull up the website that tracks queries and somehow, yes, the query I submitted four full years ago, a query that was closed as a non-responsive negative, is now labeled with not only a full manuscript request, but apparently a full manuscript was submitted. What in all the worlds?

My mind races to yesterday and the vodka-soaked email to the provost. Could I have forgotten receiving a manuscript request from my dream agent and submitting it to her? No. Not a chance. And even if that had happened somehow, there's no way Carmen would have read it already.

I type my reply with shaking fingers. Short and professional. Of course I would be happy to meet on Monday. There's no need to mention how conveniently my calendar has opened up since I declined the dean position.

I click send and stare at the screen, just waiting on something, anything, to happen. But nothing does. My room isn't filled with balloons and confetti. There's no swell of triumphant background music. My computer doesn't self-destruct like it would in a spy novel. No, it just stares at me blankly.

I re-read the emails. Carmen's and my reply. They stay the same, but everything is different.

Chapter 56

Surprise guests

The first thing I do on Sunday morning is pull up my email to make sure Carmen's note is still there. It's memorized now, tucked away with Darcy's words about my short story. *Heart-wrenching. Insightful. Provocative.*

Darcy . . .

Could he have anything to do with this? I did let him read *The Winter Mist.* And he knows Carmen . . . I could text and ask him.

But no. Not with how we left things. Was that only a week ago? I've seen him at meetings, but we haven't talked since I kissed him and kicked him out.

Andrew's right. Darcy and Olivia both deserve better than I've been giving them.

I spend the rest of the morning cleaning for Olivia's return. The bungalow is gleaming like a ring on Galadriel's finger, but something is missing. Flowers. My best friend, who just spent her birthday with her sick dad, should have flowers when she gets home. And wine. Because if I'm going to Trader Joe's, well, why wouldn't I?

I'm pulling back into the driveway, purchases acquired, when I notice a Lexus parked at our curb with two people inside.

I carry my groceries around to the front porch rather than going through the backdoor and looking through the window like a person with a normal level of concern about stranger danger. There was something about the figure behind the wheel . . .

I barely manage to catch my bag with one handle when the driver's door opens and Ash steps out.

I can't read his face. It's obvious now that Zoe is his passenger, but she's not getting out of the car. Ash says something I can't hear through the window then straightens and walks my way.

"Hey, Sis," he says. "Let me take that."

Ash takes my grocery sack from where it dangles by my side. "You crushed these flowers a little," he says, looking down at the bouquet poking from the bag.

"Ash, what are you doing here?" I ask.

He rubs the back of his neck with the hand not holding the sack.

"Do you think we could talk inside?"

I lead him up the stairs and unlock the door. "What about Zoe?" I ask as he follows me in.

He huffs a breath out through his nose, and it's such a distinctively Ash mannerism that I nearly lose it. Like, just start bawling where I stand.

"Zoe said she's not coming in until I've fixed my mess," Ash says.

"Am I your mess?"

Ash glances around at the tidy bungalow, throw pillows in place and dishwasher still running. I'm glad he didn't show up this morning, or even worse, yesterday morning, when the place was covered in tissues and half-empty cartons of take-out. He puts the grocery bag on the counter and turns towards me.

"We're my mess, Heather" he says. "This relationship. And at this point, that's my fault."

I can't help it anymore. I throw my arms around his waist and start crying into his chest. After just the briefest of hesitations, Ash wraps his arms around me. I don't remember the last time he hugged me. Maybe I've gotten an arm around my shoulder for a photo, but not this kind of hug. It probably hasn't happened since I was the taller of us.

Ash must be thinking something similar because he says "Wow, Heather. You've really shrunk."

A snort of a laugh escapes from my tears and then Ash is laughing too. Suddenly, everything is going to be ok.

Ten minutes later, I'm sitting with Ash and Zoe at the kitchen table. Olivia's flowers are proudly displayed in the center, and I've opened a bottle of wine to celebrate my brother who was lost, to me at least, and now is found. (I do have two more bottles for Olivia's return. One in honor of her birthday, another to commemorate Carmen's email. I came home from Trader Joe's well-prepared for celebration, although I myself, after the past couple of days, will be drinking very slowly, with a lot of water between glasses.)

"I never understood why you were so hard on Dad, but now I get it," Ash says.

"You're going to need to move past that too," Zoe says.

Ash makes that same huff through his nose. "I know. Just give me a day or two this time," he says. "I promise to be over it by Wednesday at the latest.

Zoe rolls her eyes my way.

"So what did he do?" I ask. "Did he try to buy you a deanship too?"

"No," Ash replies. "He wants us to move to Kansas City so I can move up within the company, but I already promised Zoe that being with me wouldn't require her to leave Denver. Dad's reply was that 'We have plenty of stray dogs in Kansas City too.' He belittled everything Zoe's worked to build."

"Well, that sounds like Harry," I say. Because, yeah, I'm still bitter.

"The two of you don't realize how lucky you are to have a dad who's willing to help you out," Zoe says. "He might not be great at it, but at least he's trying. People don't need to be perfect to be worthy of love."

Ash has been rubbing a thumb distractedly over Zoe's knuckles, but now he raises her hand to his lips. That something passes between them. The same something I see in Olivia's grin when Andrew hoists her onto his back. The same something I catch on Harry's face when my mother enters a room. The something that says "I see you and know you and love you. You're mine and I'm yours."

Darcy's face crashes through my mind. Of course it does.

A week's worth of polite smiles and attempts to tell myself that he's better off with Meredith is washed away by one gentle kiss between my brother and the woman he loves. So much for denial.

"Heather," Ash says "You still in there?"

"What? Yeah." I force a smile at him and Zoe. It's clear she knows something's up, but she doesn't push. I appreciate that.

I've just stood to go to the bathroom when the front door opens and Olivia walks inside, Andrew behind her with her carry-on.

"Whose car is that?" Olivia asks, and then she stops suddenly enough that Andrew bumps into her.

When she looks at me her eyes are flashing. "Why is he in my house?" she asks.

Oh no.

"Did you give her snacks?" I accuse Andrew.

"She didn't like anything I brought."

This is not good.

"You must be Olivia," Zoe says. She's risen and is standing between the tiny volcano and my brother. There's a smile on Zoe's face, and, is that a Twix in her hand? Where did she pull that from?

Olivia's eyes dart to the candy and then narrow.

"I followed you back," Zoe says. "On the socials." I don't imagine the wink she gives Olivia.

"Left side?" Olivia asks.

"Strong side," Zoe replies.

And then they're both laughing. Wait. How is it these two have an inside joke already?

Olivia takes the Twix from Zoe, opens it, and, to my shock, hands one of the bars back. She takes a big bite from the other.

"I guess you two are a package deal?" she asks, motioning between Zoe and my brother with the candy.

"Forever," Zoe says, putting her hand on Ash's shoulder as she bites into her side of the Twix.

"Fine," Olivia says.

And that's it. The rest of the evening passes with no drama. I listen to Olivia's news from home, and we fill her in on everything that happened while she was gone. Her shriek when she hears about Carmen Alexander would rival the nine riders.

It's only that night as I'm falling asleep that I realize I've made a decision. Whether Carmen signs me tomorrow or not, I'm taking my life off pause. Young Heather did what was right for her, but it's not right for me anymore. And maybe it hasn't been for a while. Instead of resenting her, I'm going to forgive and move on. And if that means moving into the arms of a classist (fine, he's not) Austen-obsessed professor who sees me way too clearly and seems to like me anyway, well, so be it. That's where I want to be.

If I'm not too late.

Chapter 57

Conspiritors

All right. You can do this, Heather.

I take a sip from the cup in my right hand for that extra jolt of courage, but instead of sweet pistachio I get hit in the tongue with mint. Which is fine. Mint is fine. Mint and pistachio are a classic pairing.

I allow this thought to give me hope, take a drink of the glory in my left hand, and force myself to continue down the murder hallway.

I'm halfway to Darcy's office when I hear it. A laugh, but not the high trilling type I associate with groupies. No. This laugh drives the anxiety that was inhabiting my chest to my stomach.

When I arrive at Darcy's open door, two pairs of eyes look my way. Darcy's beautiful blues and Meredith's, ugh, also beautiful blues. The objective part of me thinks about how well she fits into his world while the rest of me wonders if I could pull off a Pfisten and cover Meredith's pristine cream suit in pistachio latte.

No, Heather. Just no.

"Congratulations, Dean," I say to Darcy, plastering on my brightest smile. "I brought you a tea." I hold up my right hand as though showing the evidence. "I'm sorry, Meredith. I didn't know you would be here, and I've already drunk from this one." I bring my latte back up for another fortifying sip.

"No worries," Meredith says, a smirk lacing her smile. "I had a meeting with the Provost and thought I'd stop in to see our favorite *Dean* since I was here. But I was just leaving." With this she rises from the chair and picks up her purse. "See you later, Darcy," she says and walks past me out the door. I watch her for a few seconds as she strides away. Even the flickering lights don't diminish her loveliness. What am I doing here?

I glance at Darcy, who's straightening his already orderly desk.

Maybe I should ditch the tea and run. Back to my office hovel with my latte and my clutter.

I close my eyes and take a deep breath through my nose. No more hiding away, Heather. You are not a cave troll. You are a strong, thirty year old woman with a brother who loves you again, the best best friend on the planet and a meeting with Carmen Alexander. You don't need a man, but you want this one. Maybe even love him. You're not giving up now.

I straighten my shoulders and cross the threshold.

"Can I join you?" I ask.

"Of course," Darcy says, finally looking up. His mouth, the one I've been obsessed with for years, although I'm only now willing to admit it, is lifted at the corners in the same small approximation of a smile I've been getting at public functions all week. His eyes barely linger before looking away.

I put Darcy's tea on the desk and lower myself into the chair, aware of how much less graceful my descent is than Meredith's rise. I'm sure there's an analogy there, but I refuse to pursue it.

"So what can I do for you, Heather?" Darcy asks. At least he isn't calling me Professor Higgins.

"I just wanted to congratulate you on your promotion," I say. "We won't be sharing the basement for much longer."

Darcy lifts his tea to his lips, sets it back down without taking a sip. Runs a finger along the side where his name is scrawled in Benji's handwriting. Finally he looks directly at me.

"Why did you turn it down?" Darcy asks. "Was it because of what I said? Because I think you could have worked past that and made a very creditable Dean."

Wait. Is his discomfort because of guilt? He is benefitting from telling me about my father's nepotism, but still. That wasn't his fault. I do my best to rearrange the pieces to fit this new puzzle.

"Darcy," I say, loving the feel of his name on my tongue. Oh, what is wrong with me? "I'm glad you told me. I never wanted to be Dean. The job sounds like a nightmare. I barely want to talk to the students, let alone my colleagues or the benefactors of the college. Present company excepted, of course."

"Then why did you even apply?" Darcy asks.

"Because I didn't think anyone would be irresponsible enough to hire me," I say, retreating to flippancy.

"That makes no sense." Darcy is studying me way too closely, and I see the moment he understands.

"You really did apply just to spite me!" he says.

"It wasn't spite. More to, I don't know, tweak you? Because you didn't think I could do it."

His exasperation breaks forth in a laugh.

"Heather. Really? Of course I thought you could do it. I just didn't think you'd want to."

"Well, then you were right. I didn't want to."

Darcy sits back in his chair, legs crossed, head shaking. His smile is finally real, and it makes my burning cheeks worth it.

"Anyway," I say. "Moving on."

"Yes, of course," Darcy says, that smile still on his lips. But he doesn't say anything. Just keeps looking at me.

When the silence drags too long I blurt out "I got an email from Carmen Alexander."

"Oh?" Darcy's face shows surprise. But is it too spot-on?

"Yeah. She's interested in representing *The Winter Mist*. We're meeting today to discuss it."

"That's great news, Heather," Darcy says. Now I'm the one studying him. His smile is real, but there's something about it . . .

"Fitzwilliam! It was you!"

Darcy's hands fly into the air. "Fine," he says. "At the awards dinner Carmen commented on liking your story from *Jane, Reimagined*, but she said it was missing a spark that she looks for. I told her your passion is for fantasy, and she asked if I'd read any of your work. Since I couldn't introduce you before she left, I offered to send her your manuscript. I hope that was okay."

Okay?

"Okay?" I squeal. "Darcy, you got me a meeting with CARMEN ALEXANDER. CARMEN. ALEXANDER. Yes, that's more than okay. But why didn't you tell me?"

"I didn't want to get your hopes up if nothing came of it," Darcy says. "You deserve this chance."

My mind is reeling. I knew this was a possibility, but . . . it's so different from what Harry did. Darcy gave me an opportunity rather than buying me something he didn't think I could earn on my own. Darcy believes in me, and in my writing. He has since he first read my work, before he even knew it was mine.

"Whoa, whoa, now," Darcy leaves his chair and is kneeling before me. It's only now that I realize I'm crying.

"What's going on?" Darcy asks. "I'm sorry."

"What are you sorry for, Delancey?" I ask through a smile.

"I have no idea," he says, his smile matching my own. "Whatever it is that made you cry."

"You don't have to be sorry for that," I say. "I'm crying because you believe in me."

His look softens and I'm suddenly aware of his hands holding mine.

"Yes," he says. "I do. You're a beautiful writer, Heather. Your words bring me to other worlds and plumb the depths of my soul."

It's so over the top I can't help but laugh. "Who's the wordsmith now?" I ask.

And Darcy Delancey blushes. And oh, I love it when Darcy Delancey blushes.

He looks away and then back at me and I stare into his eyes. His gaze darts to my lips.

And then he stands. Retreats to the other side of his desk.

"I have a class in fifteen minutes," he says. "When is your meeting with Carmen?"

"This afternoon." I rise as well, picking up my work bag from the floor. "Thank you, Darcy."

"It was my pleasure," he says.

And sure, my ultimate goal wasn't accomplished, but did I really think his mouth would be back on mine this quickly? I mean, well, yeah. Maybe. But that route hasn't worked anyway. This, though. Actual communication. Real smiles. This is progress.

Chapter 58

Always meet your heroes

Carmen's office is located on the third floor of a tasteful, but not ostentatious, building complete with real plants and ivory walls. I'm sure I'm gawking like a kid on their first trip to the lake, but this is CARMEN ALEXANDER's building.

Alone in the elevator, I have plenty of time to stare at my own face in the mirrors surrounding me. By the time I leave the metal and me cube, I can feel sweat in my armpits and pressure in my chest. *This is a good thing* I remind myself. *She already loves the manuscript. The hard part is over.* My emotions have been on such a roller coaster the last week that they don't even know how to deal anymore.

And then I open the door of Carmen's office, and a blanket of peace descends. My neck relaxes. My shoulders lower. I take a deep breath, and there's no weight. What in the world?

A candle flickers on the desk before me, filling the room with a light, fresh smell. A young woman, lovely and bronze with caramel eyes, looks from the computer monitor before her and a grin covers her face.

"Heather," she says, as though seeing a long lost friend. "I'm thrilled to meet you." The woman has risen from her seat, and I realize she's even taller than I am. She speaks with some sort of accent I can't place, but it adds to the surreal feel of the moment.

"I'm Antonella, Carmen's assistant," she says. "I hope you don't mind that Carmen allowed me to read *The Winter Mist*."

The way she says it makes the title so evocative that I know I'll want to read any book she's talking about. Or better yet "Do you do voice-acting?" I ask.

Antonella's eyebrows crowd downward. "No," she says, momentarily confused. "I'm Carmen's assistant."

"Oh, I'm sorry, I know," I say. "Your voice is just wonderful. You sound like Phaenera always has in my head."

Antonella's smile returns, even bigger than before if that's possible. She's seriously a light source in an already well-lit room.

"Well, then," she says, "that is a lovely compliment."

We're grinning at each other like idiots when the door behind Antonella opens, and out steps Carmen.

Carmen looks just like I remember her from the night of the *Jane, Reimagined* awards; a middle-aged, midwestern housewife in Mary Janes and jewelry from chicos. Today she sports an orange cashmere cardigan and the confidence of Mick Jagger.

"Heather," she says, opening her arms in the universal gesture for come give me a hug. "I'm so glad you're here."

And before I know it I've allowed her soft arms to enfold me. She's at least three inches shorter than I am, not even counting my heels, but Olivia has trained me how to bend and receive love. After several seconds she gives one firm squeeze and releases me.

"Now, come," Carmen says.

Antonella gives a wave that would have looked ridiculous on anyone else over the age of four, but on her it's perfect, and I follow Carmen into her office.

At first glance her desk looks cluttered, but it soon becomes clear that there's an order to the piles. Behind her the shelves are filled with her authors' books, a framed photo beside each one of Carmen with these icons of literature.

"Now, Heather," Carmen says, pulling my gaze back from her wall of fame, "have a seat. I'm so glad you were able to meet today."

And that's when Carmen Alexander, who in the months and years to follow will become "just Carmen" to me, went from the agent of my dreams to the agent of my real life. Apparently twenty year old me, all bright and shiny and not yet cynical, knew some things after all.

Chapter 59

Happily ever after

Olivia's car is in the driveway when I get home, and I enter through the back, expecting to see her cooking or curled on the couch with Andrew. I check every room, which doesn't take long in our little bungalow, but she isn't here. Not napping, showering, nothing.

I get out my phone and text her, but there's no reply. Maybe she walked to Andrew's and they're watching a movie or something. When half an hour passes and she still hasn't replied, I text Andrew. He's still at the lab and hasn't heard from her.

I'm not going to panic. Olivia is a grown woman. Maybe she decided to walk to the grocery store. She gets crazy ideas like that sometimes. I double-check to make sure my ringer's on in case she needs a ride home.

When an hour has passed and it's getting dark, I go out to my car and start driving her normal routes. I don't see her on the way to Loose Park. If she went to the Plaza, there's no way I'll find her. Maybe the grocery? Wait. There.

I pull to the side of the street beside a figure huddled on a bus stop bench. The figure looks up, and it's her. My sweet best friend, tear lines on her cheeks.

I roll down the window. "Get in the car," I say.

Olivia's body slumps.

Glancing behind me to make sure no one is coming, I throw on my hazards and park as far forward in the bus shoulder as I can. Forget traffic laws. My best friend needs me.

I grab some napkins from the glove compartment and press them into Olivia's hand as I join her on the bench and wrap my arms around her. I can't see more than the outline of her forehead in the blinking light of my hazards, but her body is shaking. I stroke her hair and hold her close while the tears come.

Eventually she wipes at her cheeks with the napkins. When she has enough control to speak, she says "I've always wanted what my parents have. And just when I think I might have it with Andrew, they're going to lose it. And I don't think I'll be able to handle that, you know."

"Oh, sweetie," I say, pulling her back into a hug. "I'm so sorry."

A bus pulls up and slows and I wave the driver on, glad no one else has joined us at the stop.

I have no idea what to say to Olivia. There's nothing to say. We do eventually lose the people we love. A picture of Darcy flits into my head but I push it away. I'll go there, but its not the same. And right now I need to be present for Olivia.

"Your parents believe in an afterlife, right?" I ask. Olivia nods, wiping her eyes a napkin. "And I think you do too, yeah?"

Olivia nods again, sitting a little straighter.

"Then," I say, "you love people well while you can, while they're here, and you choose to believe you'll see them again after they're gone."

Olivia's face scrunches and she sniffles one more time.

"Yeah, ok," she says, nodding as she wads the napkins in one fist.

Then she squares her shoulders. I don't give Olivia the credit she deserves. Those shoulders have borne so much for me. That's what she does for people. Bears their burdens.

I pull her into one more hug before standing.

"Let's get out of here before I get a ticket," I say.

Olivia's smile is small, but genuine.

"Ice cream on the way home?" she asks.

"Of course."

That night when we get back to the bungalow with our ice cream, Andrew is sitting on the porch. He jumps up and wraps Olivia in his arms.

"Whoa, whoa!" she cries, one arm awkwardly stretched out so her cup isn't crushed. It does nothing to loosen his hold. Rolling my eyes I take the ice cream from her hand and walk past them into the house.

It's a good night for the three of us, good enough that when it comes up I admit that it wouldn't be terrible to have Darcy here. Maybe it would even be better.

"But he's with Meredith now," I say. I don't look at Andrew. "And he deserves someone who's going to treat him well."

"So you're just giving up?" Olivia asks, incredulity imbuing every syllable.

I shrug. "I'm not giving up," I say. "I'm going to intentionally build something real. A real friendship. And if Darcy ultimately chooses Meredith anyway, well, that's his choice."

A look passes between Olivia and Andrew, but I ignore it.

Chapter 60

Finally

"How did it go?"

Darcy stands in the doorway of my office, a paper cup with the logo of the cranky bean in his hand.

"Is that for me?" I ask.

He walks inside and hands me the cup. I take a sip before I answer.

"It was everything I ever dreamed a meeting with Carmen Alexander would be," I say. "She's truly a genius. Her ideas for branding me are incredible, and she's already asked to read my other two completed manuscripts."

"That's amazing, Heather. I'm so happy for you."

Darcy glances from my visitor's chair, piled high as always, to the door, but his feet stay planted.

"What's the weather like?" I ask. "I was thinking of getting outside for some air, maybe a quick walk before my next class." It's not true, but it's less awkward than asking if we should move to his not messy office.

"It's not bad out," Darcy says, "for November, anyway." He pauses before continuing. "Want some company?"

"That depends," I say. "Are you going to regale me with the differences between the Georgian and Victorian periods again?" I would let him. I'd let him talk about anything just to hear his voice.

"Not unless you want me to," he says. "In fact, I will discuss world-building or halflings or whatever else you choose."

"Such a push-over, Fitzwilliam. What's gotten into you?"

I stand and grab my coat from the back of the chair.

"That is the question, isn't it?" he says.

Once we're outside I realize Darcy may have been stretching the truth a bit to say it wasn't bad out. The clouds are low and grey, and I zip my coat, shoving the hand that isn't holding coffee in my pocket. Beside me Darcy strolls, long coat buttoned. We walk in silence for a few moments, nodding occasionally at passing students. Eventually Darcy speaks.

"Did you really not take the job because you realized you wouldn't enjoy it?"

"What other reason could there be?" I ask. I feel the air shift with his shrug. We're silent a bit longer, and as we walk I realize that I might as well tell him the truth. More than I've told already, anyway.

"The nepotism was part of it," I say. "A big part. But even without it, how could I take a job I knew I'd be lousy at when you're made for it? You actually care about the students and what they're learning. I'm just here until Carmen tells me we've got enough traction that I can quit and spend all my time writing."

"I'll miss you when you do that," Darcy says. He's still looking straight ahead.

"You'll barely see me anyway," I say. "It's not like they'll leave the Dean officing in the murder hallway."

"Murder hallway?" Now Darcy does glance my way. "Did you name it that because of how often you've wanted to kill me?"

I laugh. "No. Because of the creepy, flickering lights."

"They do add a bit of atmosphere, don't they?"

We walk a few more steps in silence.

"I didn't take the promotion," Darcy says.

I stop where I am and it takes him a minute to realize it and turn back.

"What do you mean you didn't take the promotion?" I ask. "Holy crap! I mean, it's not like I gave it up because I'm in love with you or something, but I definitely don't want Pfisten or Tweed to have it!"

The look on Darcy's face is one of my favorites. Just a little confused. Hopeful. What did I say?

"You're in love with me?" he asks.

Wait. What?

"I didn't say that."

His smile is spreading, and, oh, I want that inked on my skin. I'd stare all day. Darcy steps closer, close enough that I can smell him. In a good way. Clean and crisp and . . .

"Heather?" I look up. He's grinning. "Are you in love with me?"

"I barely even like you," I spit out.

"I know," he says. His eyes are searching mine. "But do you love me? Because I love you."

He loves me?

"Fine," I say, exasperated. "Maybe a little."

And then Darcy's hands are on my face and his lips are on my lips. I'm holding onto his coat, unwilling to let him back up even an inch. Cold water hits the back of my neck and starts rolling down the inside of my collar, but I don't care. Darcy pulls back, laughing, looks at the sky, then grabs my hand and we run towards the nearest shelter, a giant tree with branches so thick that barely any rain makes it through. And then Darcy's kissing me again and I realize the perfection of it. The rain and the tree and the man. It's a scene I would have written myself. Maybe one day I will.

I shiver just a little and Darcy pulls me close, his arms around me.

"The rain will stop soon," he says. I'm skeptical, but as far as I'm concerned, it can go on forever and I'll be happy right here.

"Crap," I say, suddenly realizing what's missing. Twenty feet away, tipped over on the ground where we were standing when the kissing began, is my pistachio latte.

"I'll buy you another when this lets up," Darcy says.

"That's ok," I say. "You don't have to."

"Well, I was responsible," Darcy says, and I can't help liking the way his eyes darken. He's staring at my mouth as he continues. "Besides, Benji needs to know that you're taken." I barely have time to laugh before his mouth is on mine again.

At some point we realize the rain has stopped. True to his word, Darcy disposes of my spilled coffee cup and takes me to the Cranky Bean for a new one. On the way I ask the question I can't banish from my mind. The one cloud covering the sun. Proverbially, because here in reality Kansas City there are about a million clouds blocking the sun. The sun could be on the other side of the planet right now for all the difference it's making.

"Do you think it will be Tweed or Pfisten?" I ask.

"Neither," Darcy says with a grin. "Once I told the provost I wasn't interested in the position, he said he'd had enough with internal applicants and wouldn't take third choice. They'll be looking for an outside hire."

"That's fantastic," I say. "Olivia and Andrew are going to be so smug. They've been calling this from the beginning."

"The outside hire?" I push Darcy gently and he grins down at me, bringing me back against his side.

"No," I say. "Us."

"They won't be too surprised," Darcy says. "Andrew may have mentioned that you were asking about Meredith."

"Oh, no. I forgot about Meredith."

Darcy laughs. "Meredith will be fine. She's actually dating the Provost."

"What?"

"Yeah. That's what she came to talk to me about when you saw her in my office."

"Well, then, Andrew should have kept his mouth shut."

"I'm glad he didn't. It was his meddling that gave me hope."

"Hope. That's it, isn't it. That's what's gotten into you."

He grins down at me, squeezes me tighter.

"That and a whole lot of happiness."

Epilogue: Tattoo 1

"And now, to toast the happy couple."

The older man who walked Zoe down the aisle stands with a microphone in one hand, a glass of champaign in the other.

"It has been my privilege to watch these two young people fall in love. They've brought out the best in each other, and I have every confidence it's just the beginning of a life-giving and joy-filled story."

The sun shines down on Zoe and Ash, seated at the head table. Beneath them Ash's dog, a furry yellow giant, part lab, part who knows what, stretches out on the grass. In fact, several dogs are in attendance with their owners. It makes me wonder if Darcy and I will have a dog one day.

I take Darcy's hand, looking down at my fiancé's first, and probably last, tattoo. A rustic latticework pattern spans his pointer finger, giving the impression that my larkspur is cradled within a basket. That's right. The obstinate man is catching my petals.

He bends down and kisses my fingers as the speaker finishes his toast. We clink our glasses in celebration and take a sip.

"You're up next," Darcy says, releasing my hand with one final squeeze for courage before I make my way to the front of the crowd.

www.ingramcontent.com/pod-product-compliance
Lightning Source LLC
Chambersburg PA
CBHW022029240626
47154CB00007B/2334